Viscount Blackwood neede[...]
only live long enough to se[...]
where better to find a woma[...]
workhouse fever ward?

Society is stunned when he announces his marriage to the unknown Miss Sarah Smith – and so is the rakish Viscount, when instead of becoming a widower he finds himself married to a lady with a will of her own. But why is she so anxious to conceal her true identity?

Soon the frail Sarah begins to occupy his thoughts far more than the luscious Lady Angela ...

The Blackwood Bride

Jasmine Cresswell

MILLS & BOON LIMITED
London · Sydney · Toronto

For Malcolm, with love

First published in Great Britain 1980 by
Robert Hale Limited, Clerkenwell House,
Clerkenwell Green, London EC1R 0HT

© Jasmine Cresswell 1980

Australian copyright 1981
Philippine copyright 1981

This edition published 1981 by
Mills & Boon Limited, 15–16 Brook's Mews,
London W1A 1DR

ISBN 0 263 73697 0

Printed and bound in Great Britain by
Cox & Wyman Ltd., Reading

PROLOGUE

The rain had finally ceased, and now the moon peered fitfully from behind the clouds, casting a pale light over the muddy waters of the river. There was little wind, although it was February, and the muted sound of men's feet hung over the mist-laden air of the embankment.

With a grunt of satisfaction, the old man dropped his sodden burden at the edge of the black water of the Thames, resting for a moment to ease his aching back muscles. His companion, muffled in the dirty remnants of a soldier's marching cape, poked at the wet bundle with his foot.

"She ain't dead," he said meditatively.

The old man cackled. "Soon will be, mate. The river'll take care o' that! It's better this way. Nor marks o' beating, that's what the man said."

"Come on then. Let's be havin' her."

The two men bent to their task, and the bundle—scarcely identifiable as the body of a woman—was swung up into their arms. The men gave of their best, and with a mighty heave the body was flung out into the centre of the muddy water. A few ripples, a slight stirring of the reeds, and then all was once again still in the cold moonlight.

The old man spat. "That's it, then. Don't let's hang about."

They slipped quietly back across the mud-flats, two dark shadows, shrouded in mist.

There was nobody to see the bundle of rags which floated to the surface of the water, and nobody to offer assistance when the shivering girl sank unconscious into the reed-infested shallows.

ONE

"Perhaps the gentlemen would like to look at the lunatics, m'lord? We have a fair parcel of them this month." The beadle paused uncertainly in the damp stone corridor, not quite sure where he should lead his exalted visitors.

"I say, Everett! A lunatic would be just the job! Why don't we come and help you choose a good one?" Sir Anthony Browne bounced with intoxicated enthusiasm.

The Honourable Jasper Clarke hiccuped gently, then fixed his companion with a quelling eye.

"You ought to *know* a lunatic would be no use. How could she give an answer to the parson? A lunatic would ruin the whole scheme."

The beadle looked alarmed. "Gentlemen . . . My lord. I understood that you had come on a mission of charity, to remove one or two lucky paupers from the custody of the workhouse."

"You understood correctly." Lord Everett, the sixth Viscount Blackwood, straightened himself up from the wooden doorpost where he had been lounging, and spoke reassuringly to the agitated beadle.

"You need only escort us to the rooms which house the female paupers. I am sure we may rely upon the matron to select a worthy object for our . . . ministrations."

The Honourable Jasper Clarke saw that the beadle's expression was still doubtful, so he plunged into speech, struggling to return his scattered wits to some semblance of order.

"The Viscount's intentions are definitely charitable, my good man. The Viscount is noted for his charitable works. Most noted. Isn't that right, Tony?"

Sir Anthony Browne, not sufficiently inebriated to feel comfortable about telling an outright lie, blinked several times, well aware that the Viscount watched him cynically.

"The Viscount's intentions are certainly honourable," Sir Anthony said at last, peering at the beadle rather nervously.

This seemingly innocuous remark struck the Honourable Jasper as exceptionally humorous, and he chortled noisily for a moment or two. The Viscount glanced at him briefly, a suspicion of impatience tightening the hard line of his jaw.

"Take Jasper to look at the lunatics, there's a good fellow, Anthony. I think I shall achieve my purpose more swiftly if only Dr. Thompson accompanies me."

Sir Anthony and Jasper took no offence at this summary dismissal, and lurched off down the corridor in high spirits, weaving sporadically from side to side of the narrow work-house hallway.

The beadle, who had been a kind-hearted man before time and the nature of his work exacted their toll, watched the erratic progress of the two gentlemen with quiet irritation. He could not refrain from thinking that several of his old madmen behaved no more strangely than the two men saun-tering about the hall, but his poor old lunatics were kept chained to the wall. He sighed, and craned his neck upwards to look at the Viscount and the physician who accompanied him. At least *this* nobleman seemed relatively sober, and the doctor reassuringly respectable.

"I shall escort you to the female wards, m'lord," said the beadle. "You'll understand that we're a bit crowded just at the moment, on account of all the fever in the parish. To be honest, it'll be a regular godsend to get even one of the sick ones taken off our hands."

The beadle stopped outside a forbidding oak door, its sturdy panels reinforced by an iron bar which was padlocked to the stone wall. He coughed apologetically as he unwound the chains.

"We have to keep the males and females apart, m'lord.

It's regulations."

He rapped sharply on the heavy door which was opened, after considerable delay, by an old woman whose strength seemed scarcely sufficient for the task. She appeared overcome by the sight of the beadle, and stared at him with frightened eyes, her hands clutching nervously at the dingy grey stuff of her skirt.

"We done everything you said, sir. 'Tweren't our fault the sacks wasn't sewed. More than half of us is sick, sir, and 'tis hard to do the work for two. Do we still get our dinners, sir?"

"Shush, Hetty. I haven't come about the sewing. There are two gentlemen here to see the matron."

"Gentlemen?" Hetty peered out into the gloom of the dark corridor and saw the tall figure of the Viscount. She dropped an awkward curtsey, responding instinctively to the innate authority of his silent presence. She curtsied again, less deeply, to the physician.

"Come with me, sirs. The matron will be in her office."

The beadle bowed low to the Viscount. "I will leave you, my lord, if I may. I must find your companions before they become completely lost. I will ask them to wait for you in my rooms. The matron can tell you and Dr. Thompson all that you wish to know about our female inmates. My own duties are chiefly with the male paupers."

"Thank you." The Viscount's voice was cold, but polite. "I am obliged to you for your help."

"It's a pleasure, m'lord. It's hard for the poor people in London. There's nobody to look out for them here like there is in the villages. We don't usually get noblemen like yourself on a visit."

For the first time, a flicker of emotion was discernible on the Viscount's face, but he said nothing, merely bowing slightly to the beadle before turning back to the old woman.

"Perhaps you will conduct us to the matron's office immediately? My carriages wait below and I cannot keep the horses standing much longer in this weather."

"Yes, sir. My lord." She hobbled off at a brisk trot, beckoning to indicate that the distinguished visitors should follow. Now that her dinner was secure, her step seemed quite jaunty. She paid no attention when the heavy door clanged shut behind the beadle, and the narrow corridor sank into almost total darkness.

Their journey to the matron's office was fortunately brief. The stench which assailed the Viscount's nostrils several times threatened to overcome him, and he was obliged to keep his eyes fixed rigidly on the ground ahead in order to avoid tripping over the huddled figures which hunched list-lessly against the damp stone walls. He was now completely sober for the first time since receiving the lawyer's letter four days ago, and he was suddenly assailed by doubt as to the wisdom of his project. Resolutely, he shook off his uncertain-ties. He needed a woman on the point of death, and where better to find her?

The matron's office, though shabby enough by the Vis-count's usual standards, seemed a haven of comfort after the chill dankness of the rest of the workhouse. The Viscount moved immediately to the fire, grateful as much for its comforting red glow as for its warmth. Dr. Thompson looked round sourly, his expression dour. He remained as silent as before.

Mrs. Gresham curtsied deeply, flattered to receive such elegant gentlemen in her room. Unlike the beadle, she was not burdened by any undue sensitivity or by an overly kind heart. She saw no reason to exert herself keeping feckless paupers alive when common sense indicated that everybody would be better off if they were dead. Her plump bosom and rosy cheeks had misled many a well-meaning churchwarden as to the true nature of her character; but some instinct warned her immediately that neither of these visitors would be easily deceived.

She smoothed her cap over her grey curls, and deftly concealed a bottle of gin behind a convenient cushion. The elder of the two visitors looked as if he might be one of the bothersome new Methodists, and there was no point in looking for trouble.

"How can I help you, sirs?" she simpered coyly. "Was it about the shipment of girls going to the Bahama Colonies?"

"No, it was not. I am Viscount Blackwood. This is Dr. Thompson, my physician." His voice was curt. "I have the beadle's permission to visit the female sick ward." He knew the brief explanation was inadequate and not likely to satisfy the avid curiosity he saw lurking in the matron's sharp little eyes. He tried to expand his explanation.

"I have decided to choose one or two paupers and remove them to one of my estates. Dr. Thompson will attempt to treat their ailments. At the very least, the paupers I select will be able to ... expire ... in comfort."

He felt sickened by the hypocrisy of his apparent charity. For a moment he wondered if thwarting his father was sufficient justification for compromising his personal code of ethics. Now that he had seen the conditions prevailing in the workhouse, he was no longer sure that he wanted to take advantage of any woman forced by her circumstances to die in such miserable surroundings. Then he remembered Lady Angela, and his resolution was renewed.

During his brief silence, the matron looked at her visitors speculatively, wondering what profit there might be for her in this strange visit. She did not, of course, believe a single word of the Viscount's explanations. A man less likely to be moved to charitable visitations and good works was hard to imagine. Mrs. Gresham might preside over the female wards of a workhouse in London's dockyards, but she recognized a member of the *ton* when she saw one. But there was, she decided rapidly, no possible advantage to be gained from laying difficulties in her visitors' path. She pulled the heavy bundle of keys from her desk, and bustled towards the door. Her expression was at its most motherly.

"Well, and I'm sure it's more than kind of you, sir, to think of my poor lonely paupers. Why, only this morning I was saying to our surgeon—such a dedicated man!—that I didn't know where to turn for another pallet or a bit of blanket. It's been a cruel winter, sir, and there be poisonous vapours clear over the whole city. Going down like flies, they are in this parish. The Vicar can't hardly find time to bury them all, and that's a fact. And the ground so hard, it takes three of the beadle's healthy paupers just to dig the pit . . . that is to say, the grave."

She changed the conversation rather hurriedly. "Was you wishful of old women, or young ones, my lord? We've got them with babies, and without."

The Viscount flicked open his snuff box and inhaled deeply.

"I must know their names," he said stiffly. "And I do not wish for a baby. Otherwise their age matters little to me."

"Well, they've all got names, my lord. That's one thing we can give 'em free!" Mrs. Gresham chuckled cheerfully. "Even the little 'uns left on the doorstep gets a name."

She stopped outside a narrow doorway, and gestured towards it uncertainly.

"This is the fever ward, my lord. Are you sure that you want to go in? Perhaps the doctor is more accustomed . . .?"

"I wish to go in myself." The Viscount's answer cut short her hesitation. He walked swiftly past the nauseating rows of pallets, wondering how on earth he was to make his selection.

Dr. Thompson interrupted the Viscount's silent examination, speaking almost for the first time since their arrival in the workhouse.

"It would be unreasonable, my lord, to expect your servants to nurse the victims of virulent or contagious fevers."

"Do all these women have the fever which is now raging in the city?" the Viscount asked the matron.

"Most of 'em, my lord." Mrs. Greyham stepped gingerly across the threshold of the door. She was usually at considerable pains to avoid entering the fever rooms, leaving all the sick-room tasks for the healthy paupers. She pointed to one of the straw mattresses.

"Lizzie here has been in the workhouse for years. I don't think she has the fever, my lord." The matron peered at the old grey face and shrunken body which lay quite still on the dirty pallet. "I think she's still alive, my lord. Anyway, she were alive at dinner-time yesterday. They always manage to wake up for their food."

"She's alive," agreed Dr. Thompson. "Looks as if she's dying of old age and starvation. She doesn't have the fever. Not yet, at any rate."

"Then have her carried to my carriage," said the Viscount curtly. His eyes searched the dimly-lit room and fell finally upon the face of a young woman, pushed into a far corner of the ward.

"Who is she?" he asked. "She seems younger than the rest of your inmates."

"That one was fished out of the River Thames last night, m'lord. Ours was the closest parish, so they brought her here. Sarah, she said her name was. 'Spect she was starving and decided to end it all. She didn't have a penny on her, and wearing nought but rags."

"Why, then, is she in the fever ward?" asked the Viscount, with some curiosity. "Since she still lives, cannot she be fed and returned to a state of health?"

Mrs. Gresham looked at him pityingly. "Lor, bless you, m'lord. I don't suppose she'll last out the night. When you're starving and go into the river in February, you don't live to tell the tale to your children. It's a miracle she's still breathing now. The Parish don't pay us to feed the ones that are going to die. There's more than enough to feed who are fit and well."

The Viscount cast the matron one sharp look, before he walked to the young woman's side. Mrs. Gresham, sadly conscious of a failure in her motherly façade, hastened to join him, tucking the single blanket more securely around the emaciated figure of the young woman. The Viscount stared silently at the white cheeks which rested on a scrap of torn calico, noting dispassionately that the woman's brown hair was matted and still tangled with small clumps of water weed. Her hollow cheeks were sunken, her eyes were closed. If it had not been for the sharp rattle of her shallow breaths, it would not have been possible to tell that she still lived. He reached under the thin cover, and pulled out the woman's hands. Her bare fingers were bloodless, and icy cold.

"I wish to speak to her," he said to the matron.

"But, m'lord, she's dying! She can't speak!" Mrs. Gresham's voice revealed her aggravation. Whatever this strange man's motives, her chances for personal profit seemed increasingly slim. If he took Sarah and Lizzie away, she would not even be able to claim the parish burial allowance.

The Viscount looked up from the bed. "I think some spirits would revive her. I expect you have some gin." His voice was flat, without a trace of emotion, but Mrs. Gresham shivered.

"I might just have a drop of daffy somewhere, m'lord. I keeps it especially for occasions like this one."

"I thought you might." The Viscount's smile failed to reach his eyes. "I shall also require a glass of drinking water."

Mrs. Gresham hurried out of the ward, her rosy cheeks quivering with disapproval. She'd have a good nip of gin before she brought her bottle back to be wasted on a woman who was probably no better than she ought to be. Glass of drinking water, indeed! They hadn't given Sarah anything since she'd been brought in yesterday, so why should they start now? Here was a fine way to be encouraging women who went around throwing themselves off river banks. Mrs. Gresham sniffed virtuously. She retrieved her bottle from behind the cushion and sipped it lovingly. Not many matrons, she thought tearfully, would be so willing to sacrifice their belongings for the sake of a mere pauper.

The Viscount took the bottle from Mrs. Gresham's grimy hands with only the most perfunctory word of thanks, and tilted the rim against the young woman's bloodless lips. Most of the gin splashed on to her chin, before trickling down her neck and soaking the filthy mattress. At the second attempt, however, some of the liquid must have reached her throat, for she spluttered slightly and her body twisted under the thin cover. The Viscount rested his hands behind her neck and shoulders, pulling her up into a sitting position. Her eyes flickered briefly open and then closed again as her body went limp.

"Sarah!" Gently, the Viscount flicked her on the cheek. "What is your full name, young woman?"

"Sarah," she repeated dutifully, her eyes still closed. "Sarah Jane Smith."

"Can you open your eyes, Sarah? I would like to help you, if I can."

"Water. Want water." Her voice was a pathetic croak, a mere thread of sound.

The Viscount gestured to Dr. Thompson, who came over to the bedside, his face rigid with distaste.

"Here, young woman. Drink this." Dr. Thompson's voice was gruff, but his hands were gentle as he rested the glass against the girl's mouth, his hands moving to feel the feeble beat of the pulse in her wrist.

She drank the water gratefully, and this time her eyes flared open in recognition of her surroundings. "Why am I here? Who are you?"

The doctor touched her forehead, smoothing the wild disorder of matted hair out of her eyes. Her hands remained icy, her body—still wrapped in the shabby clothes she had worn when found in the river—burned with heat. Dr. Thompson's eyes met the Viscount's and, almost imperceptibly, he nodded his head.

He turned his attention back to the woman on the bed.

"I am Dr. Thompson. You have been unconscious for a while. Do you have a husband or some family whom we could ask to take you away from here?"

"Cassie's dead. Uncle Charles is dead, too." The words cracked over the parched dryness of her throat. "Please don't leave me here."

The doctor spoke briskly. "If there is nobody else . . . My—er—friend has come to take you away from here. You can come with us, if you would like to try and get better."

"Shall I get her carried downstairs, then, my lord?" asked Mrs. Gresham ingratiatingly. "I don't think she could walk, poor little thing."

"Yes, yes." Now that the selection had been made, the Viscount seemed impatient to be gone. The doctor could sense his urgency to get away from this horrible matron and the hellish fever ward with its aura of death. The Viscount turned away from the bed.

"I will wait for you in my carriage, Dr. Thompson. I shall rely upon you to make whatever arrangements you think suitable or necessary."

"Yes, m'lord."

The doctor looked down at the patient who had just been assigned to his care. The stench of decaying river weed mingled inextricably with the indefinable odour of death. He saw Mrs. Gresham, rubbing her hands together in a parody of concern for the unconscious girl.

"I suppose there could be very few things worse than dying in here."

TWO

Viscount Blackwood adjusted the folds of his cravat with infinite patience. Satisfied at last, he reached out to extract a large sapphire from the jewel box at his side. His fingers hesitated, poised over the stiff creases of white muslin. Sir Anthony Browne could tolerate the silence no longer.

"Dammit, Everett! You know you cannot go ahead with this. Think of your reputation, if you do not care for your family!"

The Viscount paused in the act of inserting his tiepin. His face, reflected in the mirror, expressed exaggerated concern.

"Good lord, Anthony, I myself thought the effect was rather pleasing. And surely we should not allow ourselves to overestimate the importance of our dress?" He smiled slightly. "I acknowledge that there may be two opinions about the suitability of sapphires, but surely the family honour can hardly be considered at stake?"

Sir Anthony refused to be diverted. "You know very well that I meant nothing about your tiepin, Everett, so don't try to turn me aside with your glib tongue. We were drunk this afternoon, all of us. We should never have gone to the workhouse. Jasper and I would never have borne you company if we hadn't been three parts castaway."

The Hon. Jasper Clarke stirred uneasily. "Anthony's right, old fellow. Bad business, this. Thoroughly bad business. Not to say that your father was wise making that deuced ridiculous will. But better to marry one of the gals you know and have done with it. Stands to reason, old chap. You can't go rushing off and marry some hag out of a workhouse just to annoy your father." He thought deeply for a moment or two. "Besides, your father's dead. No way of telling he'd be annoyed now. Then where will you be? Stuck with a woman from the slums, and no way of getting rid of her."

The Viscount turned from the long looking-glass, finally satisfied with the disposition of his jewelled pin.

"Come, come. You are both faint-hearted all of a sudden. Besides, you have forgotten the most important part of our plan. I do not intend to take on a wife. I plan to become a widower. Then, when my inheritance is secure, I can marry the woman of *my* choice. Dr. Thompson has examined the girl again, and says she is starving, has congestion of the lungs, and will scarcely survive the night. I can be married this evening and celebrate my freedom in the morning."

Sir Anthony, not much given to profound moral reflection, was surprised to detect an unpleasant queasiness somewhere in the region of his stomach.

"But the girl, Everett. Surely it's not right to take advantage of a woman on her deathbed."

The Viscount spoke impatiently, perhaps to conceal his own uncertainties. "You did not see the fever ward, my friend, and I did. You may take my word for it, that I have done Sarah Smith an inestimable favour in removing her from St. Katharine's Workhouse."

"If she is so near death, then how do you expect her to play her part in the wedding ceremony? How do you know that she will be willing? That she isn't already married?" Sir Anthony shook his head sadly. "Everett, let's admit that we were drunk and have done with the affair. Dr. Thompson is already stiff with disapproval and you have not told him the half of your plans. What do you imagine the Vicar will say, when you drag him out in the middle of the night to perform the ceremony?"

"We are wasting time," said the Viscount curtly. "Your objections are without foundation, Anthony. *I* was not drunk this afternoon—at least not for a large part of it. You seem to have forgotten that we are in London. I could have found half a dozen clergymen willing to marry me to the devil himself provided that I produced a special licence and five pounds for their pockets. As to the rest of your worries, well, you may come with me and hear the girl for yourself. I imagine that Dr. Thompson will have made her as comfortable as possible by now. She lies next door, I believe. We may enter through my dressing-room."

The Honourable Jasper was shocked. "Can't put her in your mother's old room, Everett. Not the thing. Not the thing at all."

The Viscount's expression was cynical. "Come, Jasper. Did you not realize that you were about to witness the culmination of a touching love affair? You have not yet appreciated even half my powers of invention. Come along, let us go and inspect my bride."

The room which they entered was softly lit by the glow from several candles. The tall windows were hung with pale gold curtains which matched the heavy silk draperies around the four-poster bed. Propped up by three or four pillows, the young woman seemed without life, her light brown hair tumbling around a face of deathly pallor. Only on her high cheek-bones, two small patches of fiery red indicated the fever that burned through her body.

Dr. Thompson looked up as the three men entered the room. His expression was stern, his whole attitude tense with disapproval. He bowed slightly to the Viscount.

"You see, my lord, that I have fulfilled your orders. The old woman has been taken downstairs to the servants' quarters and given some gruel. Her chief problem seems to be chronic underfeeding. The young woman has been washed and made as comfortable as possible."

"Thank you." The Viscount's voice made no concession to the doctor's evident censure. "How is she?"

Dr. Thompson shrugged. "There is no hope that she will survive the night. I am not sure that I will even be able to bring her to any awareness of her surroundings. She should never have been left in those wet garments, and of course her body is wasted by starvation. She has no strength to fight for her life."

As if to give the lie to the doctor's words, the girl in the bed stirred slightly, and her lips twisted into a tortured grimace. "Water . . . give me . . . please."

The hoarse words were scarcely audible, but the Viscount crossed swiftly to her side and lifted her gently from the pillows. He held a glass of lemon water to her bloodless lips, shocked—although he gave no sign of this—by the dry heat that burned through the linen of her borrowed bedgown.

"I have some lemon water for you, Sarah," he said quietly. "If you drink it, you will start to feel a little better."

The girl in the bed made no answer, but gulped noisily, almost desperately, at the cool liquid. When the glass was finished, her tense body relaxed slightly against the Viscount's arm. "More," she whispered. "I need more."

The Viscount looked doubtfully at the physician. "Is it wise for her to drink so much, Thompson?" He looked down at the pale face resting on his arm. "She seems a little more lively now."

The doctor shrugged. "Nothing that you do will have much effect one way or the other, my lord. If your purpose with the young woman is . . . what I suspect . . . you had better get the business finished as quickly as possible. This may well be her last burst of consciousness before the end."

"Thank you for your advice." The Viscount smiled grimly. "I will relieve your professional conscience, Thompson, by suggesting that you go downstairs and ask one of the servants to provide you with a meal. Perhaps you would also be good enough to ask the housekeeper and two of the serving-girls to come up to this bedchamber immediately? I do not want the events of the next hour to pass by without some witnesses."

"Very good, my lord." Dr. Thompson walked silently towards the door, his back rigid with unspoken disapproval. At the doorway he turned, unable to contain himself any longer.

"My lord!" he burst out. "Can you not reconsider this ill-advised scheme of yours? I have known you since the day of your birth, and I know what happens when you get the bit between your teeth. But this is not the answer, my lord. Indeed it is not!"

The Viscount's expression hardened momentarily, but his answer was mild.

"I have no notion what you are talking about, Dr. Thompson. As I believe I mentioned to you early this afternoon, I am engaged upon a mission of charity. My father's lawyer has suggested to me that my life style is strong in debauchery and weak in good works. I plan to rectify the imbalance."

"As you say, my lord. I will summon the housekeeper. Perhaps you would also like me to send up the clergyman whom I observed waiting in the hallway?" He made no effort to conceal the sarcasm underlying his question.

"That would be most helpful." The Viscount's voice and face remained bland. "Good evening to you, Dr. Thompson."

The door had no sooner shut behind the doctor, than the Viscount poured out fresh lemon water for the dying girl, and urged her to drink.

"Sarah," he said abruptly, "Can you hear me? Can you understand what I am saying?"

The girl opened her eyes, and with an obvious effort focused them upon the man by her side. The Honourable Jasper and Sir Anthony moved closer to the bed. This was the first time any of the men had seen her fully conscious.

The girl shuddered convulsively. "The river . . ." she croaked at last. "They were going to put me in the river."

Her eyes glazed with remembered terror, and she collapsed again into unconsciousness.

Jasper looked at her warily. "She don't look very rosy, Everett. Maybe we should call back Dr Thompson."

"Jasper's right, you know," agreed Sir Anthony. "The woman's too sick for a wedding tonight. You'll have to give up your scheme for today, and try and find somebody a bit healthier tomorrow."

The Viscount replied patiently, as if making a familiar point to a group of difficult children.

"I do not wish for somebody healthier. If I wanted a wife, I could choose any one of a dozen young society virgins. I have explained to you until I am quite tired of it, that I wish to become a widower."

He looked up at his friends, registering their doubtful expressions and spoke quickly, his voice raw with exasperation.

"For heaven's sake! You cannot pretend that I am doing this woman any disservice. Look at her surroundings at this moment—and remember from whence she came!"

He turned back impatiently to the girl. "Sarah! You are quite safe now. You must wake up. I have to ask you to perform a small service for me."

Sarah opened her eyes again and, with an evident struggle, looked at the Viscount. Her cheeks burned with fever as she visibly forced herself to concentrate on the man by her side.

"Where am I?" she whispered at last. Her throat was still parched from the days without food or water. Dimly she remembered the inky blackness of the Thames as it closed over her head, and the unbearable, penetrating cold of the workhouse.

"They're all dead." She did not realize that she murmured the agonized thought out loud, although she half-sensed the quick look that flashed between the two men standing at the end of her bed.

The Viscount propped her upright against the soft pillows, removing his arm so that he too could stand up and observe her from a slight distance. To the girl, the tall figures loomed distant and menacing through the haze of her fever.

"I am Viscount Blackwood." The tallest of the three men introduced himself with a slight inclination of the head.

"These gentlemen are two of my friends. Their names are Sir Anthony Browne and the Honourable Jasper Clarke, but you do not have to trouble yourself to remember that. Sarah, we have taken you from the workhouse where we found you, and we have tried to make you comfortable. In exchange, I wish to ask you for a small favour."

His voice was tight with self-loathing, as he started to form his request. To the girl in the bed, it seemed that he spoke with all the hauteur and authority of generations of aristocratic power.

"Yes, my lord." The habit of obedience was instinctive. "What must I do?"

"I wish you to marry me," said the Viscount calmly. "I have a clergyman waiting belowstairs who is prepared to perform the ceremony tonight."

"Marry you, my lord?" Sarah's response was languid. The Viscount's request was so bizarre that she felt certain the fever was distorting her comprehension, twisting some sensible, commonplace remark into the silly request she seemed to have heard.

"Yes. I must marry quickly in order to comply with the terms of my father's will." The Viscount's words were hurried, impatient. "I need to be married before the end of this week, and so I am asking you to become my bride."

He did not add that he intended to be a widower rather than a bridegroom. There was no point, he assured himself, in burdening the mind of a dying woman with the thought of her imminent death.

It was still an effort for Sarah to think, and even more of a burden to speak. She smothered an hysterical laugh, which emerged from her fever-wracked frame as a choking gasp. Her uncle had obviously worried in vain about his niece, abandoned to the goodwill of his parishioners. How long since he had died? One month? Two? Already she was on the brink of matrimony. The weak laughter bubbled up again, her mind sliding off into the nether world of semi-consciousness.

"Oh yes, my lord. I should like to marry you, of course."

She sank deeper into the pillows, closing her eyes but still aware of the murmur of voices all around her bed. She realized at last that she must be dying, and she spared sufficient energy to marvel at the false clarity of her deathbed visions. Even the smell of the workhouse had faded, to be replaced by a pleasant combination of candle smoke, fresh herbs and the expensive perfume of her imaginary trio of gentlemen.

"What was your name?" she muttered. "The one I am to marry?" The weak, helpless laughter rippled through her body. She hoped desperately that this vision would not fade, returning her to the harsh, cold reality of the workhouse fever ward.

"I am Blackwood," said the cool voice she already remembered. "My full given name is Everett Giles Carlton Blackwood. I think you told me your name is Sarah Jane? Sarah Jane Smith?"

"Yes," she whispered, pleased that her dream had not gone away. Perhaps, after all, dying alone would not be so bad. But the fever betrayed her once again.

"Smith!" she exclaimed softly. "That's such a lovely *commonplace* name."

"Dammit, Everett!" Sir Anthony could not contain himself any longer. "Let's get the parson in here and get this over with. I cannot stand much more of it. It's monstrous . . . inhuman."

The Viscount crossed unhurriedly to the door and gestured to the people gathered in the small hallway outside the bedchamber.

"You may come inside now."

He spoke to the housekeeper as she tiptoed past him into the sickroom. "I have asked you here so that . . . my betrothed . . . may have some females to bear her company. There is an attachment between Miss Smith and myself which is of long standing. At my earnest entreaty, she has consented to honour me by going through a ceremony of marriage. As you can see, Miss Smith is . . . very sick."

Mrs. Benson looked solemnly from her employer to the pale figure propped up in the bed. A romatic at heart, she was torn between delight at participating in such a deathbed wedding ceremony, and sentimental sorrow that the Viscount's wedded bliss was likely to prove of such short duration.

She looked significantly at the maids, then nodded her head sagely. "Mary and Eliza and me is wishful of offering our respectful good wishes," she said.

The Viscount smiled poitely at the housekeeper, and managed to look as though he struggled to contain an unbearable sorrow. He hoped fervently that, for once, the uncanny intuition of his servants would not flush out the whole secret. He spoke softly.

"Thank you, Mrs. Benson. I can only regret that Miss Smith's scruples prevented our marrying sooner. Now it is almost too late."

Sir Anthony and the Honourable Jasper stared at their friend in considerable astonishment, and the Viscount turned to speak to the parson quickly, before his housekeeper could think up any awkward questions. At any moment, somebody would notice the absence of his mother, the Dowager Viscountess, and then there would be no end to the awkward questions.

"You have come prepared with the necessary papers?" he asked the parson.

Parson Jakes, whose natural curiosity was considerably dulled by the enormous quantity of gin he had consumed since receiving the Viscount's advance payment of a golden sovereign, nevertheless felt a spark of interest at this hint of thwarted romance. But, having taken a good look at the Viscount's icy face, he ventured no impertinent questions. Bowing low, or as low as he felt was safe, bearing in mind the liquor swirling through his system, he smiled ingratiatingly.

"The certificates are all in order, my lord. They merely require names and signatures to correspond with those written on the Bishop's special licence."

"I will write out our full baptismal names," said the Viscount briefly. "You will require them during the ceremony."

The parson felt himself warmed by a glow of kindliness, only partly inspired by the gin, and looked with paternal benevolence towards the pathetic figure in the bed. Well acquainted with death—a familiar visitor in his poverty-stricken London parish—he needed no words from the Viscount to convince him that the bride hovered on the brink of death. He crept over to the bedside, clearing his throat in nervous anticipation of the ceremony ahead. It was a good many years since he had last found himself in such opulent surroundings. He leant over the bed, searching the dim recesses of his memory to recapture the priestly manner that had once been his greatest source of pride.

"Well, my child. I have come to assist at your marriage." He cleared his throat again, wishing that he might have the courage to ask for a nip of gin. There was a tension in the atmosphere of this room which was rendering him distinctly uncomfortable.

"Father!" The young woman's eyes fluttered open, and rested fleetingly on the clergyman's clerical collar and shabby black suit. "Father!" she exclaimed joyfully. "You have come to take me to heaven!"

This evidence of Miss Smith's pious nature, and her awareness of the imminence of death, reduced Mrs. Benson and the two maids to a state of tearful sentimentality. Jasper, however, was overcome by quite other emotions.

"That's torn it," he whispered to Sir Anthony. "Did you hear that? 'Father' she said. She's probably a Papist—one of the Irish immigrants. D'you think its legal when a Church of England parson marries a papist?"

"Of course it is," said Sir Anthony robustly, in a voice that quite failed to carry conviction. "Besides, Everett ain't a papist, and the girl isn't going to live long enough to make a protest."

They subsided into a glum, uncertain silence. Everett must be half out of his wits, they decided, to insist upon marrying this girl about whom they knew absolutely nothing. Frustration over the terms of his father's will had driven him outside the bounds of what was rational.

The Viscount ignored the restless glances of his two friends and, having completed the certificates, he now planted himself squarely at the bedside of his supposed fiancée. He wanted no more attempts at polite conversation, and did not wish to risk any more potentially embarrassing revelations from the woman he was to marry.

"Miss Smith is very weak, as you can see," he said to the clergyman. "It would be better if you married us as swiftly as possible, so that we do not tax her strength unnecessarily."

He took Sarah's hands within his grasp, and said brusquely, "We have Sir Anthony Browne and the Honourable Jasper Clarke to act as witnesses. Mrs. Benson will offer her arm to support my . . . bride. You may proceed with the ceremony."

Jasper stared anxiously at the girl in the bed, but her eyes remained opened and apparently aware of her surroundings. The parson searched in the pockets of his faded clerical coat, and produced a somewhat tattered copy of the Book of

Common Prayer. He opened the volume with hands that trembled slightly.

His voice stumbled hurriedly over the familiar phrases of the opening exhortations, only slowing slightly when he reached the crucial point of the exchange of vows. He looked at the wraithlike bride, her head resting on the housekeeper's arms, her expression dreamy and faraway.

He spoke more sharply than he intended, afraid that she would fade away before he could pronounce the final words of union.

"Repeat after me: 'I, Sarah Jane, take thee, Everett Giles Carlton . . .' "

Her voice, faint and thin, repeated the promises after him. Her eyes, staring unseeingly into the distance, seemed focused upon some vision denied to the other occupants of the room. Mrs Benson's hiccupping sobs punctuated the ceremony at regular intervals, and Sir Anthony discovered that he was holding his breath as though in anticipation of some frightful emergency.

There was a concerted sigh from the onlookers when the Viscount removed his great signet ring and pushed it gently over the wasted fingers of his bride. It hung limply on her slim hand, an enormous lump of solid gold against the bloodless pallor of her skin.

Parson Jakes wiped a trickle of sweat from his brow and beamed happily. He had performed his task, and four more golden coins now awaited him. At twopece a shot, he could buy sufficient gin to last him a year or even—marvellous thought—a bottle of real brandy. He smiled again at the Viscount.

"Well, my lord, the knot is tied. You have only to sign the papers. And the new Viscountess, too. She signs Miss Smith for the last time, isn't that so, my lord?"

There was silence for one or two seconds, before the Viscount and his friends all rushed into speech. All three of them realized at the same moment that a pauper from the workhouse would almost certainly be illiterate. Sarah Smith was probably accustomed to marking her name with an "X", if indeed, she had ever previously been called upon to sign a document.

The Viscount's voice finally overrode the incoherent splutterings of his friends.

"You must give the quill to me," he said calmly. "Naturally, I shall have to assist the Viscountess in this task. Her strength is not great enough to support a pen."

He gestured to Sir Anthony to bring pens and ink, then sat himself on the bed alongside his bride. Carefully he lifted the icy white fingers, suppressing all visible signs of the emotion that flickered through him at the featherlight touch of his wife's hand. The quill was handed to him, and he wrapped her fingers around the shaft.

With a violent movement, she wrenched her hand from his grasp, a scream of terror shaking her body.

"No!" she panted. "You shall not make me do it. I will not. You may *kill* me before I will sign." Her eyes, no longer focused on the distant vision, flamed with passionate rage as they stared at the Viscount.

"I may be innocent of your world, sir, but I am not stupid. I shall *never* sign!"

She collapsed against the pillows, her body wracked by shuddering breaths as she struggled to draw air into her lungs.

"My lord!" The parson was horrified at this sudden crumbling of his rosy interpretation of the scene in the bedchamber. "My lord! You gave me to understand that this ceremony was the consummation of a long-standing attachment. As a man of the cloth, I cannot countenance a forced marriage."

The Viscount turned to him impatiently.

"The marriage was in no way forced upon Miss Smith. You saw yourself how willingly she made all the responses. Besides, the deed is now done and her signatuture is merely a formality. Can you not see that her mind wanders? She is in a delirium. Did I not tell you that there were reasons why we could not wed before? Her mind has gone back to . . . gone back to the circumstances of her own family situation."

Sir Anthony heaved a sharp sigh of relief at his friend's quick thinking.

"Indeed, sir," he said to the parson. "You need not trouble yourself about this marriage. I myself heard Miss Smith agree with the Viscount that she wished to be wed. Just before your entrance into this room, Miss Smith was quite lucid and seemed eager for the marriage to occur."

The parson thought longingly of his bottle of brandy. He looked reluctantly at the helpless figure on the bed, quiet now under Mrs. Benson's soothing hands. The Viscountess would be dead by the morning, and his four guineas would last for a year. He shrugged his shoulders. The brief struggle with his conscience was over.

"Very well, my lord. If you would be good enough to sign both your own name, and that of her ladyship? In the circumstances—in view of the Viscountess's health, I am sure your signature will be acceptable."

The Viscount removed a small pouch from his pocket and inclined his head ironically towards the parson.

"I am pleased that your judgment coincides with my own," he said blandly. The purse slipped easily from the Viscount's hand into the parson's upturned palm.

"I'm sure my butler will be happy to offer you some refreshment before you return to the duties of your parish."

Parson Jakes, his fingers clutching the satisfactorily solid purse, backed out of the bedchamber, bowing profoundly to anybody happening to meet his glance. The door closed softly on his rapidly retreating footsteps.

Mrs. Benson looked up from her ministrations at the bedside.

"She's awful quiet, my'lord." The housekeeper recollected the new status of her patient, and amended her words.

"That is to say, her ladyship appears to be ... er ... sinking, my lord." She sniffed loudly. "And her so beautiful once, I've no doubt."

The Viscount cast a swift, startled glance at the unconscious figure of his new wife.

"I wish to be alone," he said at last. "Mrs. Benson, perhaps you would be good enough to see that Sir Anthony and the Honourable Jasper are given something to eat before they retire for what's left of the night." He smiled, a genuine smile that lit up his face with a hitherto unsuspected charm.

"I'm afraid it's been a long day for us all."

Japser attempted a mild remonstrance.

"Can't leave you alone, Ev. Not the thing at all. Tony and I will bear you company."

The Viscount looked at his friends from beneath hooded lids. His expression was inscrutable.

"I wish to be alone with my wife, Jasper. Thank you for your generous offer, nevertheless."

Sir Anthony shuffled his feet uncomfortably.

Well, of course, Everett, if that's what you prefer, Jasper and I will say no more. We shall see you tomorrow morning, no doubt?"

"No doubt," agreed the Viscount tranquilly, and watched the small line of servants and friends troop out of the bedroom door. His gaze flickered back to the girl on the bed and, as if attracted by the intensity of his regard, her eyes came open.

"What? Still here, my lord?" The girl laughed weakly, her eyes appraising the Viscount's elegant appearance with frank approval.

"I'm glad I imagined *you*," she said softly. "You're a nice dream." Her hands tautened on the fine linen of the sheets, and a quiver of panic fled across her face. "You won't let all this go away? Promise me you won't! I don't want to go back there."

The Viscount took hold of her agitated hand.

"I promise," he said quietly. "I promise that you shall not go back to the workhouse." He touched the burning cheeks, watching the sweat trickle down into her tangle of brown hair.

"I do not think, my lady Viscountess, that you will be going anywhere."

THREE

A young footman flung open the door to the breakfast-room, causing Sir Anthony Browne and the Honourable Jasper to look up from their silent consumption of cold roast beef and devilled kidneys. The Viscount, freshly shaven but with his face still ravaged by traces of exhaustion, came quietly into the room. He slumped down at the table, saying nothing until a footman attempted to place some ham on the empty plate in front of him. Impatiently, he ordered the servant away, staring morosely at the flames which leapt around the coal heaped in the fireplace.

It was Sir Anthony who broke the grim silence.

"Er . . . how is everything, Everett? That is, I mean to say . . . the girl. Is she . . .?' He coughed awkwardly. "Sarah—has she passed away?"

The Viscount turned from his contemplation of the fireplace. A bitter smile twisted his mouth.

"Why no, Tony. Your congratulations are in order! Lady Blackwood has survived the crisis. Dr. Thompson is with my *wife* now, and he assures me that with nourishing food and complete rest, there is no reason why she should not recover completely."

He looked at the horror registered on his friends' faces, and laughed harshly as he paced up and down the room.

"Well, aren't you ready to congratulate me? Do we not have something to celebrate? Instead of finding myself a widower this morning, I find myself the proud possessor of a new Viscountess! You, of all people, will understand how admirably suited I am likely to find her for that rôle."

Angrily he turned to one of the footmen. "Bring me some burgundy and then clear out of here, all of you! Tell the rest of the servants that I am not to be disturbed—not for any-thing—is that understood?"

"Yes, my lord." The servants withdrew in discreet silence. They knew better than to cross his lordship when he went into one of his moods. Sir Anthony, Jasper and the Viscount were left staring at one another across the gleaming surface of the table. This time it was Jasper who broke the tension-filled silence.

"You remained with . . . er . . . Lady Blackwood yourself last night, Everett?"

"Oh yes!" The Viscount laughed mockingly. "I felt it was my duty, you know. After all, I had married the woman, the least I could do was remain at her side until the end."

"What happened?" Sir Anthony's question was brusque. "When we left the room she was on the point of death. Why does Dr. Thompson now tell us that she will recover?"

The Viscount shrugged. "Dr. Thompson is not very communicative this morning. He is too busy tending his patient with cordials and nostrums. And any spare energy which he has, he is devoting to pointing out that he warned me not to risk marrying the girl."

"But dash it all, Ev.! She had congestion of the lungs, and a raging fever. Her hand was weaker than a newborn kitten's paw! Now you tell us she survived the crisis. What *happened* during the night?"

The Viscount pushed back his chair, tossing off another glass of burgundy before walking over to the fireplace and staring moodily into the depths of the burning coals.

"If we had left her in the workhouse, of course she would have died. If I could have brought myself to ignore her cries last night—then she would have died also. But I found myself unable to resist her pleas for water; when she strug-gled for air, I lifted her up; when the sweat poured from her brow, I applied cool cloths." He shrugged. "In short, I played the rôle of loving nurse and now I am rewarded with the life of my patient."

Sir Anthony reached for the decanter of burgundy.

"There has to be some solution, Everett. You must see Witherspoon and ask him about an annulment. Surely it could be arranged?"

"Are you run quite mad?" asked the Viscount wearily. "After all the gossip and scandal that has attended our family since the terms of my father's will became known, do you think I am about to subject myself and my mother to such a scandal as *that* would cause? Good God, man! An annulment probably requires an Act of Parliament for a peer, just as a Bill of Divorce would do. And why would I subject myself to this? I still could not marry Lady Angela. I still could not inherit my father's fortune. You know I had only four days left under the terms of his will."

"Then what do you plan to do, Everett?"

"I shall see Witherspoon and claim my inheritance." He smiled bitterly. "I have no doubt I shall find it considerably easier to think about my future when I am cushioned by the knowledge that several thousand pounds sterling are lying in my bank account." He looked at his friends, then laughed harshly.

"Since I have found myself wedded to a whore from the slums of London's dockyards, I may as well enjoy a last expensive fling before I am forced to withdraw from society."

"We don't *know* she's a whore, Ev." Jasper spoke cautiously. "Could be a respectable woman, down on her luck. Can't all be whores down at the dockside. Not enough men to go round.

The Viscount's mouth twisted into a smile.

"Why, there is a cheerful thought! With luck I may find myself wedded to the virgin daughter of an illiterate stevedore! How perfectly she will be suited to a life as Viscountess Blackwood! Should I present her first at one of the queen's drawing-rooms, or should I merely aim for vouchers to Almack's?"

He threw his glass on to the stone hearth, grinding the delicate pieces of crystal beneath the heel of his riding-boot.

"On the whole, gentlemen, I think I should prefer a whore. She will find her morals perfectly in keeping with the rest of my acquaintance."

He nodded briefly to the two silent men.

"I will bid you good-day, for the present. I find that pressing business calls me to my lawyer's office. But I believe we shall meet tonight—at Lady Angela's, is it not?"

He turned round from the doorway and laughed cynically.

"I shall be relying upon you to help me celebrate in bang-up style. It is not every day that one of us marries!"

Mr Witherspoon greeted his noble client with a deferential bow. While the senior clerk busied himself ushering the Viscount into the room's most comfortable armchair, Mr. Witherspoon set out a decanter of brandy and two large glasses. Beneath the cover of a polite exchange of views on the weather and the health of the Dowager Viscountess Blackwood, the lawyer examined his client's forbidding expression with considerable wariness. Viscount Blackwood could not, by the wildest stretching of the imagination, be considered an easy person to advise and today his humour looked especially precarious.

Mr. Witherspoon had already spent an exhausting eleven months explaining to the Viscount why his father's will could not be overturned. In the eyes of the law, the will might be considered eccentric, but its validity was beyond question. Old Viscount Blackwood had left the lands of the family estate in strict accordance with the terms of the original entail. He had therefore been perfectly at liberty to dispose of his other income, jewels and personal property in any manner that he wished. It was simply unfortunate for the present Viscount that the entailed land was of little value, whereas his father's personal assets produced, an income of several thousands of pounds each year. Mr. Witherspoon had spent many a weary afternoon trying to convince his noble client that the will might well be unreasonable, but unreasonableness did not render it illegal.

The lawyer sighed quietly and offered the Viscount a second glass of brandy. He feared that this interview—taking place only four days before the Viscount lost his inheritance—was going to be more difficult than any which had gone before. Seating himself behind the comforting familiarity of his broad desk, Mr. Witherspoon tried to speak firmly.

"Well, my lord, I wrote to you last week and told you that our last appeal to overset the terms of you father's will had failed. Therefore, it is now my duty to remind you that in four days' time I shall be compelled to turn over the residue of your father's assets to Lord Frederick Babbington. Lord Babbington is, of course, your father's designated heir should *you* fail to marry in accordance with his wishes."

Mr. Witherspoon shuffled his papers to cover the uncomfortable silence. He knew how bitterly the Viscount chafed under the public humiliation of his father's will. He saw how the Viscount's hand clenched around the delicate stem of the brandy glass, and a gleam of sympathy came unbidden into his eyes.

"My lord," he said with unaccustomed mildness. "You must attempt to resign yourself to the facts of the situation." The lawyer hesitated for a moment, then shrugged his shoulders as he plunged into speech.

"Try to understand your late father's frame of mind, my lord. Your brother was killed in the Peninsula, leaving no heirs. You yourself are well past your thirtieth birthday and—forgive me, my lord—notorious for your passage through the gambling-halls, drawing-rooms and . . . er . . . bedchambers of London society. I regret very much that the last Viscount chose to state in his will that you could only inherit his personal estate if you married within the year. I regret even more that your father stated expressly that you could not marry Lady Angela Thorpe unless you were prepared to forfeit your inheritance. But these things are done, my lord. The terms of your father's will are facts which must be accepted."

The Viscount rose to his feet, and looked at the lawyer with cold eyes. His voice was thickened by disgust.

"As you have pointed out, Witherspoon, I am well past my thirtieth birthday and accustomed to conducting my personal affairs outside the light of public speculation. My . . . relationship . . . with Lady Angela Thorpe had caused sufficient scandalous gossip even before my father decided to give written foundation to the scurrilous rumours circulating throughout London society. When Lady Thorpe became a widow three months before my father died, I was honour-bound to marry her. We waited simply so that she might fulfil the year of formal mourning for Sir Henry Thorpe's death. The speculation as to what I would do now that Lady Thorpe was a widow had hardly died away before the terms of my father's will became public knowledge. I will leave you to imagine *my* feelings at the dishonour my father offered to the woman I wished to marry."

Mr. Witherspoon looked squarely at his client.

"I attempted to remonstrate with the late Viscount," he said. "During your father's last illness, I pointed out to him that you had an . . . obligation . . . to Lady Thorpe. Your father, my lord, was very frank on the subject of your obligation. I can see him now, my lord. He simply snorted with something of his old vigour and said, 'Think I don't know what the young hothead will feel honour-bound to do? That's why I wanted the clause in the first place. Doesn't matter to me what Everett says about me after I'm not here to listen to him.' "

Mr. Witherspoon returned his eyes to the papers on his desk.

"I could not budge your father from that position, my lord."

The Viscount splashed brandy from the decanter into his

glass, with reckless disregard for the polished surface of the table.

"I did not come here to discuss my father," he said curtly. "I have come to inform you of my marriage."

He tossed a collection of papers down on the desk in front of the lawyer.

"I believe you will find the certificates in order."

With trembling fingers, the lawyer retrieved a marriage certificate from the slim package of papers. His eyes flickered over the name of the bride, and a shudder of relief ran through him. The old Viscount's gamble had paid off. Sarah Jane Smith. An undistinguished name for the wife of Viscount Blackwood, but at least the young fool had not married Lady Angela Thorpe. Witherspoon tried to gather his scattered wits.

"My lord, this is certainly most unexpected news! You gave us no hint of your intentions when we saw you only ten days ago." He permitted himself a beaming smile.

"And most happy news, of course. I offer you my felicitations, my lord. I am delighted at this joyful outcome, as I'm sure all your friends must be."

"A joyful outcome indeed," said the Viscount cynically. He laughed at some inner thought, and then turned a bitter face towards the lawyer.

"I shall look forward to the moment when I can introduce you to my bride."

"I shall be honoured, my lord."

"That remains to be seen. Perhaps when you meet with the new Lady Blackwood you may wonder if you were wise to act as my father's accomplice in drawing up that infamous will."

"I was scarcely an accomplice, my lord." Mr. Witherspoon spoke with quiet dignity, not attempting to unravel the meaning of the Viscount's cryptic remarks.

"As I have just told you, I attempted on several occasions to have the offensive clauses removed from your father's will.

The former Viscount was adamant in his insistence that they should remain. I am merely an advisor, my lord. I could not dictate the terms of your father's will."

The Viscount brushed his hand across his forehead in a weary gesture.

"You are perfectly right, of course. I know that you have always done your best for me, Witherspoon. But I cannot pretend that I am happy to find myself married when I have been publicly forbidden the wife of my choice."

The lawyer regarded his client steadily.

"I have known you, my lord, since you were in short coats, so you will have to forgive me if I speak frankly. The remark you have just made will serve no useful purpose. You should take care not to repeat it outside the confines of this room." He cleared his throat uneasily.

"We both know, my lord, that there has been . . . conjecture . . . concerning the possibility of your marriage. We must hope that your bride can be introduced into society in a way which will give nobody any cause for further gossip. I am sure, since you decided to take such a sensible step, that you have been wise enought to select a young lady whose breeding and manners are alike impeccable. The time has come to put a stop to the endless scandals associated with the Blackwood family name."

The Viscount remained silent for two or three tense seconds. Then he laughed briefly.

"I do not think that I am ready for any further homilies today, Witherspoon. Your good sense always reduces me to an uncomfortable mood of self-doubt." He rose to his feet and stood tall, almost overpowering in the low-beamed office.

"Just let me have some of the funds which are now mine. I must settle some debts before I leave London. I think I am planning to take my . . . wife . . . into the country."

"You will no doubt benefit from a period of quiet relaxation. Although perhaps it is not entirely wise to remove from

town so soon after taking the plunge into matrimony . . .?"
The lawyer hastily corrected the slightest impression of
rebuke.

"I shall make sure that the funds are paid into your
account at Coutts' by Thursday morning. I hope you will
find that time enough?"

"I have waited for almost a year. Thursday morning will
be time enough." The Viscount nodded politely to the
lawyer.

"I *am* obliged to you, Witherspoon, for your assistance in
the past, although it may not always have seemed that way."

"Our firm is honoured to be of service to the Blackwood
family, my lord. Please be so good as to convey by respectful
good wishes to her ladyship, your bride."

The Viscount's lips thinned into a tight line.

"Lady Blackwood will no doubt be honoured to receive
your message."

He bowed briefly and was gone.

FOUR

It did not require an eye as experienced as Potter's to see that Viscount Blackwood was considerably under the weather when he strode into his town house some time after three in the morning. His boisterous night on the town with Sir Anthony and the Honourable Jasper had done little to alleviate his overwhelming sense of gloom. He could only be grateful that social conventions prevented his seeking a few moments alone with Lady Angela Thorpe. There would be time enough for that painful interview when his own feelings were a little less raw.

The butler, unwise enough to make some innocuous remark about the improved state of Lady Blackwood's health, very nearly had his head snapped off by his furious employer. The Viscount, having discarded his greatcoat, scarf and gloves in a trail from the entrance hall to the library, sank into an armchair and showed no signs of heading for the comforts of his bed, despite the lateness of the hour.

As soon as he was provided with a large decanter of brandy, he paced up and down the library floor, managing to consume sufficient alcohol to leave him less than steady on his feet, without having any very desirable effect upon the general state of his temper. Alternately cursing fate and his father, he tried hard to avoid dwelling on the lowering truth that the major part of his troubles sprang from his own actions.

Tormented alternately by memories of Angela's soft body pressed into his arms, and visions of his mother's likely reaction when he presented her with the disastrous facts of his present situation, he felt himself overcome by waves of destructive rage the like of which he had never previously experienced. Seized by a mood of murderous self-disgust, he stormed up the stairs to the room where he would find his wife.

The chambermaid did not need to stare long at the Viscount's scowling brow and sneering mouth to know that her employer was in a towering rage. Curtseying fearfully, she did her best to shrink into invisibility. The Viscount did not bother to spare her a second's glance.

"Get out!" he said briefly.

Curtseying again, the maid backed to the door, relieved that she would not have to remain alone in the room with such an evil-visaged monster. There was some mystery attendant upon the Viscount's marriage, as everybody in the servants' hall knew. Whatever the true facts were, they seemed to be having a disastrous effect upon the master's temper. As she confided to her room-mate when she was safely back in the distant servants' attics, the Viscount in one of his black moods fair gave her the shivers. She wouldn't fancy being married to *him*, not for all his title and grand houses.

The Viscount, who had no clear idea why he was standing in his wife's room at three in the morning, stared angrily at the sleeping figure of his bride. One of the maids must have brushed her hair, and it now flared out in a soft cloud of dull brown, around the sunken hollows of her cheeks. His signet ring still rested on her finger, although it was hard to believe that such a frail hand could support its weight. Her thin body hardly made a curve in the smooth surface of the covers, and the Viscount shuddered silently as he compared the wasted limbs of this girl with the voluptuous beauty of Lady Angela. Deliberately, he thrust all thoughts of Lady Angela aside, and walked reluctantly over to the bed. He realized, with a sigh of regret, that he was once again stone cold sober. Alcohol was offering him little relief tonight.

"Well, madam," he said harshly to the sleeping girl.

"How do you like your new rôle as a Viscountess? Better than plying your trade down at the wharfside, I'll be bound."

He saw the slight movement of her hands, and jerked away impatiently. He had no wish to wake the woman, no real wish to talk to her. There would be time enough to explore the full degradation of his position. In fact, for the first time in his life, he was aware of a bewildering lack of purpose in all his actions. With one brief ceremony last night, it seemed that he had shut himself off from all contact with the world he had previously known. The path for his future led mistily into the unimaginable.

"Where am I? Why am I here?" The hoarse whisper from the bed interrupted his disillusioned self-examination, mocking the uncertainty of his own mood. Irritated, he turned round and saw that the girl—impossible to think of her as his wife—had opened her eyes. She lay as still as ever, but her enormous grey eyes gave an animation to her face that had previously been lacking.

The Viscount looked at her coolly. He was too much in the habit of masking his emotions to permit his unhappiness to show.

"I trust you remember me," he said tersely. "I am Viscount Blackwood." He tried to say, "I am your husband, the man whom you married last night," but the words stuck in his throat.

Sarah pushed a bewildered hand across her forehead. The light in her grey eyes dimmed a little and her voice, when she spoke, was weary.

"I thought I was really awake this time, but you're still here." Her hands stroked the soft linen of the sheets, and with an evident effort she turned her face to rub her cheek against the lace of the pillows. Her face tightened with panic.

"It's all so real. I think perhaps I must be going mad." She fixed her eyes upon the Viscount and spoke to him fiercely.

"Come here! Come closer! I wish to touch you."

The Viscount came readily and sat down on the bed. He took Sarah's hands into his own clasp and stared intently at her haggard face. A suspicion, which had lurked half-formed ever since the wedding ceremony, suddenly crystallized in his mind.

"Who are you?" he asked sharply. "Where do you come from?"

Sarah's weak laugh was drowned in a spasm of coughing. When she had recovered her breath she looked at the Viscount and shook her head reprovingly.

"You have the rules all wrong, my lord. Visions cannot interrogate their creators. I am supposed to ask *you* questions, not the other way about."

Impatiently the Viscount took her shoulders and raised her body until she stared directly into his face. He could feel the sharpness of her bones through the thin fabric of her bedgown.

"Look at me, Sarah!" he commanded. "You know that I am not a vision. You can feel my hands holding you—they are real hands. You were in a delirium, but that is past now. You have had no fever since early this morning. Your day has been spent almost entirely in sleep, I believe, and although you may feel confused, you are now awake. You are not dreaming."

"Then I am truly in this comfortable bed? I am not in the workhouse any more?" She turned to look wistfully at the cup of milk that stood on the table by her bedside.

"The milk is real, too? I may drink it without ruining the dream?"

"Of course." The Viscount handed her the cup, watching dispassionately as her trembling fingers guided the cup to her lips. She tried to disguise her eagerness, but the milk slid down her throat in famished gulps. She turned her eyes away from the Viscount when the drink was finished. She spoke without meeting his gaze.

"I was afraid to take it before, in case it wasn't really there.

Usually, when one is hungry, it is safe to imagine anything one pleases, as long as you don't try to pretend that you're eating."

The Viscount forced down a flicker of emotion, which he refused to identify as pity.

"I understood that Dr. Thompson arranged for you to be given some gruel. In your present weakened state he naturally could not feed you more substantial meals."

Sarah hastened to answer the implied rebuke.

"Oh! I'm sure the doctor gave me the gruel. It's just that I am hungry, having been without food for so many days. And then, I am still confused as to what has actually happened and what is the product of my imagination. You would not believe *some* of the stories my fever invented for me last night!" She flashed the Viscount a rather shy smile.

"Besides, I am always hungry, you know. My sister complains that I have enough appetite for two hungry dockporters."

The Viscount frowned, but made no immediate comment. The painful thinness of her body did not suggest that she was in the habit of indulging her hearty appetite very frequently. When he finally spoke, his voice was deceptively mild, containing a note of bland enquiry that would have set any of his servants instantly on guard.

"I must tell you, Sarah, that my curiosity has been increasing ever since I came into this room tonight. I don't know how much you remember of the events of the last few days, but perhaps I may be allowed to refresh your memory. You were found in the fever ward of St. Katherine's Workhouse. St. Katharine's is a parish situated in the very heart of London's dockyards, an area not renowned for the gentility of its inhabitants. I was given to understand by the workhouse matron—and the wet rags you were wearing bore out this information—that you had been rescued as a destitute suicide from the banks of the River Thames." He smiled in a fashion that sent a small chill down Sarah's spine.

"You will realize that I became intrigued when I discovered that the object of my charity, far from being the illiterate, unmannered drab whom I might have anticipated, turned out to be a young woman of obvious education."

He looked piercingly at Sarah's ashen face. "Could you explain to me, Sarah, why a woman fished out of the river after an unsuccessful attempt at suicide, should turn out to be possessed of an education far beyond her apparent station? Do you realize that in all the conversations we have had, you have never once committed an error in grammatical construction? Your accent alone marks you as a member of the educated classes. I cannot think how the three of us managed last night to miss the significance of your manner of speech."

There was no response from the silent woman in the bed, and the Viscount looked down at her restlessly.

"Well, Sarah. I await your answer."

She did not respond to him, lying with closed eyes under the heavy canopies of the bed, apparently dead to the world. Seized by a curious urgency, the Viscount placed his hand around her wrist. The pulse beat strongly beneath his fingers. Roughly, he jerked his hand away.

"You may desist from this convenient play-acting, madam. You are no more unconscious than I am. I feel entitled to know who you are. You may console yourself with the thought that it is unlikely that your crime can exceed my worst expectations." He spoke dryly. "As your husband, I am likely to share your desire to keep your past offences concealed, if it is at all possible."

Her eyes flew open with startling rapidity.

"My husband!" she repeated dazedly. Her hand clutched at his sleeve. "Then I didn't imagine the whole? There really was a wedding here in this room last night? A parson came?" Her grip on his sleeve tightened. "Then . . . then what is my name now?"

Gently the Viscount removed her hand from his sleeve. He

took the time to brush away an imaginary crease.

"That, if you will remember, is what I have just asked *you*, my dear."

The girl in the bed could not hide the parade of emotions which ran across her face. Bewilderment, a flicker of amusement, followed by fear, overwhelming and blotting out everything else.

"I am Sarah," she said at last. "I must have told you this yesterday. I am Sarah Jane Smith."

"Well, yes. Those are indeed the names which appear on our certificate of marriage. But, off-hand, I can think of at least two other ladies whom I know who share with you the name of Sarah Smith. As you mentioned last night in an unguarded moment, it is such a splendidly *commonplace* name, is it not?"

He smiled again, the cold smile that froze Sarah's hands into rigid claws, clasping the sheets for protection.

"I would like to hear your life history, my dear. As your husband and protector, I feel it is no more than any due." His glance sharpened into open mockery.

"You will find me all considerate attention."

Her eyes slid away, to examine the fingers toying nervously with the bed linen.

"There is very little to tell you, my lord. My sister and I were left as orphans at an early age. We were taken in by the minister of our parish and treated in every way as if we had been his own daughters. My sister Cassie and my . . . guardian . . . were both victims of the recent epidemic fever which has been sweeping the poorer sections of the city."

"Why, that is an admirably brief autobiography, Sarah! And, moreover, it possesses the tremendous advantage of showing you as the innocent victim of harsh circumstance. I can only admire such quick thinking, my dear. And in your reduced state of health, as well!"

Sarah bit her lip. "It was not quick thinking, my lord. It was the truth."

"But it nevertheless omits some points which I am forced to consider rather interesting. As your husband, you know, I confess to an insatiable curiosity concerning the *precise* chain of circumstance that led up to your decision to end it all in the river."

"Why did you marry me, my lord?"

"That does not answer my question, Sarah."

Her voice was weak, but she looked at him steadily.

"*I* did not ask *you* to marry me, my lord. As you must know, I was delirious last night and quite unaware of the consequences of my words and actions. I see no reason why I should reveal details of my personal history to a man whose integrity must surely be very much in doubt."

"If my integrity is truly in doubt, it would certainly be wiser not to goad me with provocative speeches. Come, Sarah. I am now responsible for your future. May I not share some of the details of your past?"

Sarah sank back against the pillows, seeming suddenly more frail, more shrunken than she had before.

"There is no great mystery, my lord. Our . . . guardian . . . was poor and dedicated, often a fatal combination for a lowly clergyman without connections. His stipend as vicar of St. Stephen's was usually spent before it was received in caring for the destitute of the parish. When he died and my sister with him, I found myself utterly alone and without funds. Do you find it so strange that I decided to end a struggle that had become unbearably burdensome?"

"I think, Sarah, that you have told me only some of the truth. And it is the omissions from your story which I find more interesting."

A faint flush crept into Sarah's cheeks, but she said nothing more. Her body was racked by a sudden fit of shivering, which she tried to conceal from the Viscount's determined scrutiny. He found himself touched by this evidence of pride as he would not have been by any spurious pleas for mercy.

He rose to his feet, astonishing himself by his own forbearance.

"Very well, Sarah. I will not press you for more information tonight. But we are going to have to exchange confidences at some time, you know. After all, we are now committed to one another for the rest of our lives, and we must resign ourselves to many years of one another's company. An awesome thought, is it not?"

"You do not have to endure my company," said Sarah tartly. "I cannot imagine why you married me, my lord, but you need not fear that I shall take advantage of the situation. Indeed, I should prefer to remain independent."

She was struck by a sudden thought, and struggled to sit up more firmly in the bed, her face lit by a glow of eagerness.

"Perhaps you would like to provide me with a small cottage somewhere in the country? I would go away and never trouble you again, my lord. I would change my name . . . make no claim on you. With a garden and a cow, I could live on a very small income."

The Viscount smiled cynically.

"An idyllic picture, my dear. You are suddenly *most* accommodating. And just what is your definition of a 'very small income'?"

She did not hear the sarcasm of his question.

"Would fifty pounds a year be too much?" She could hardly breathe because of the nervous tension. With fifty pounds, she could afford to take Aggie with her. She stole a glance at the Viscount and, misunderstanding the blankness of his expression, collapsed against the pillows. Her breath escaped in a sad little sigh.

"We have managed on less, of course, my lord. I did not intend to appear demanding."

"That is enough! Be silent!"

The Viscount was furious to discover himself shocked into sympathy for this derelict from the workhouse. Fifty pounds and a cow! The last piece of lace which he had given to Lady

Angela had cost a hundred pounds, twice the amount this girl asked for to last her a year.

The Viscount, who had been brought up to accept the enormous disparity between his own situation and that of the vast mass of people around him, was aware of an unfamiliar sensation of guilt. His manner of living ensured that he was rarely exposed to the harsh struggles of the underprivileged, and he was uncomfortable at this close, personal contact with hardship and privation. When he spoke, his voice was brusque as he tried to maintain his usual note of languid indifference.

"You must rest, madam. I shall return tomorrow morning so that I may inform you what steps I plan to take in order to rectify this situation." His eyes rested briefly on the thin, white face of his wife.

"Good-night, Sarah. Do not waste the next few hours in inventing stories for my delectation. I am not a gullible man, and I shall discover the truth eventually, you know. You must endeavour to conserve your strength."

Her eyes fluttered open for a moment, but closed again before she had time to observe the faint softening of her husband's expression.

"I shall ask one of the maids to sit with you, Sarah. If you require something to drink, or some other service performed, you should not hesitate to ask." He laughed, as if at some private joke.

"You are, after all, the new Viscountess Blackwood."

FIVE

The Viscount breakfasted early the next morning, consuming generous quantities of ham and coffee while ignoring the bottle of madeira that the butler had thoughtfully provided. He appeared to be in an unexpectedly mild humour, a fact which the under-footman hastened to carry back to the kitchens. The servants began to hope that the disturbing—and mutually conflicting—rumours which they had heard concerning the new Viscountess would, after all, prove to be without foundation. When the Viscount voluntarily sought out his secretary, the servants sighed with relief. It was common knowledge that Mr. Jeffries had been led a merry dance over the past year, since the Viscount refused to participate in the administration of the Blackwood estates, and even declined to sign any documents related to the part of his inheritance which was in dispute. The master, they told one another hopefully, must at last be preparing to assume the arduous duties and responsibilities of his rank.

Mrs. Benson, who was the first to observe the Viscount's entry into the secretary's small office, nodded with satisfaction and hurried off to discuss this interesting turn of events with the butler. A firm believer in the beneficial effects of Romance and Matrimony, the housekeeper was delighted to pass on this solid evidence of the Viscount's reformed character. Potter, listening approvingly to the news, condescended so far as to agree that the Viscountess was undoubtedly the cause of this unprecedented conference.

This, in fact, was the case, although not at all in the manner imagined by Mrs. Benson and Potter. The Viscount's visit to his secretary was motivated solely by suspicion concerning his bride. Plans for a reformed life style could hardly have been further from his mind.

Finding his secretary deep in earnest perusal of the morning's political news, the Viscount tapped him courteously on the shoulder. He always felt guilty that Jeffries should suffer the brunt of the inconvenience caused by the late Viscount's idiosyncratic will. Mr. Jeffries, whose dedication to the Viscount's interests was exceeded only by his solemnity of manner, sprang to his feet. A guilty flush stained his wrinkled cheeks, as if he had been discovered dallying with the kitchen-maid, rather than improving his mind by pondering affairs of state.

"Lord Blackwood! Sir!" His voice contained as much enthusiasm as he would ever permit himself to show. "May I offer you my hearty felicitations, sir, on this happy occasion?"

"Why, thank you, Jeffries. I am touched by your exuberance. Do you really consider my visit to your offices merits such extravagant congratulations?"

"I spoke of your marriage, sir." Jeffries did not try to disguise his disapproval of the Viscount's levity. As far as Mr. Jeffries was concerned, life was a serious affair, and should be treated accordingly. He spoke severely. "Then perhaps you have come to approve the recommendations contained in my report on the agricultural improvements at Wrexham?"

"Alas, Jeffries, I am afraid not. I am forced to confess that I did not know such a report existed."

"I included it in the last set of papers sent to you for signature, sir."

The Viscount appeared lost in contemplation of his finger-nails.

"But you already know, Jeffries, that I do not read documents concerning my father's estates. You are authorized by my father's lawyers to administer the property as you and they see fit. My father did not choose to make me his heir. You cannot expect me to show particular interest in administering the trust."

"Yes, my lord. But I did just think—now that you are married, you know—that you would be interested in Wrexham again. It has reverted to you, after all."

The Viscount looked up from a leisurely inspection of his left hand.

"Ah yes," he said meditatively. "My recent marriage. I knew there was some reason why I had come to see you today." He smiled faintly. "Other than for the pleasure of your company, of course. Now that you mention my marriage, you have brought this little matter to mind. I have recently become curious about a certain parish in the East End of London, situated near the dockyards. If I remember correctly, the parish is called St. Stephen's, and I am particularly interested to learn whatever I can about the last incumbent. A very dedicated man, I am given to understand, who was supported in his charitable works by two young ladies."

"You wish to make enquiries about this parish, sir?" Mr. Jeffries was understandably bewildered. "Or did you wish to know more about the vicar?"

"Both the vicar *and* the parish, I think," said the Viscount. His attention appeared to wander, but with difficulty he brought it back to the matter under discussion.

"And, of course, Jeffries, anything you can find out about the two ladies would be . . . er . . . most useful."

"Yes, my lord." Mr. Jeffries was so rarely asked to do anything at all by the Viscount that he felt he could not pass any comment on this somewhat peculiar task. He had been in Lord Blackwood's service since the day the Viscount came down from university, but he had long ago abandoned any hope of understanding the complex motivations which moved the Viscount to action. A week ago he would have sworn that his employer was still hopelessly infatuated with Lady Angela Thorpe, a mercenary harlot in aristocratic clothing if ever Jeffries had seen one. Now it transpired that the Viscount was married to an unknown girl—and apparently, if rumour was to be believed, after months of secret romance.

"I fear that employment with me has its difficulties, Jeffries." The Viscount's voice held a hint of laughter as it broke into Mr. Jeffries's thoughts. "Never mind. May I rely upon you to send an unexceptional announcement of my marriage to the Morning Post?"

"Naturally, sir. I have already drafted a few lines for your approval."

"Admirable, Jeffries. Wherever should I be without you?"

The Viscount smiled with real warmth, ignoring his secretary's air of somewhat flustered disapproval.

"And console yourself with the thought, my friend, that your report on St. Stephen's is one which I shall read with the greatest attention."

The Viscount rang the bell for the butler.

"My hat, coat and gloves if you please, Potter. I must pay a call upon the Dowager Viscountess."

He glanced at his watch and smothered a yawn. "Not yet ten in the morning and I am already forced to go out for an appointment. Marriage is a most fatiguing business."

"Yes, my lord." Potter's response was at its most wooden. He gestured to the footman carrying his lordship's outer garments, and personally helped the Viscount ease his shoulders into the multi-caped greatcoat.

"Mrs. Benson wished to ask your lordship when Lady Blackwood's luggage might be expected to arrive. We have been unable to find any personal attire for Lady Blackwood anywhere in the house, my lord."

"Good lord, luggage!" The Viscount frowned distractedly, then shrugged. "Lady Blackwood's belongings will be arriving shortly. Perhaps this afternoon," he said smoothly. He accepted his gloves and hat from the butler, tucking his cane beneath his arm. The butler bowed low, but looked at his employer knowingly as he reached the door.

"I'm sure Mrs. Benson will be pleased to hear about the luggage, my lord."

The Viscount turned back, looked at Potter searchingly, then smiled ruefully at his secretary.

"I cannot imagine why you bother to ask my advice about anything, Jeffries. It is perfectly clear that my servants know far more than I do about what goes on in my household."

Mr. Jeffries seized his courage with both hands.

"The remedy for that situation lies within your own grasp, my lord. If you would but turn your mind to it, we both know that you *could* be the ablest administrator the Blackwood estates have ever known."

"Another lecture, Jeffries? I am keeping tally, you know. That is the sixth which I have received in the last two days. For some reason, all my friends—not to mention the members of my household—seem determined to impress me with the benefits of their wisdom. Let us hope that my mother has not effected a similar transformation and become anxious to reform me overnight."

"It seems an unlikely possibility, sir." Jeffries permitted his mouth to twist into a small, dry smile. "Please be so kind as to convey my respectful good wishes to the Dowager Viscountess."

"Beneath that superficial gloominess of manner, Jeffries, there undoubtedly beats the heart of an unregenerate optimist. You have known my mother for upwards of thirty years. Whatever leads you to suppose that I shall be able to silence the Dowager long enough to say *anything* coherent—let alone pass along other people's polite messages?"

The Viscount stepped out cheerfully into the rigours of the February morning, without giving his secretary a chance to reply. The butler and Mr. Jeffries were left to stare after his retreating back with varying degrees of bafflement and hope.

The Dowager Viscountess Blackwood was bored. She yawned upon her elegant day-couch, wondering disconsolately how she was to survive another single week of mourning for her late, occasionally lamented, husband. Staring into the mirrors lining the wall of her boudoir, she twitched the froth of lace that served as her apology for a widow's cap, and tugged with unladylike vigour at the black silk of her gown. Life as a widow was very flat.

The sounds of an approaching visitor, even one calling at such an impossibly unfashionable hour, jolted her into a pleasant state of eager anticipation. Disposing her glorious dark curls in their most becoming clusters, she turned round to welcome her visitor. At the sight of her eldest son, she flung herself off the couch and into his arms with a total disregard for convention and the dictates of female decorum.

"*Everett!*" cried the Dowager in a muffled shriek of astonishment, which suggested that she had not seen her eldest son in months, perhaps years. "Where have you been? And how could you leave me all alone for *weeks?*"

Laughingly, the Viscount disengaged himself from his mother's embrace, looking into her eyes with an affectionate smile that had never been seen by any of the other women who passed through his life, not even Lady Angela.

"Come, come, Mama. I seem to recall that you forced me here for that horrendously dull dinner party not ten days since."

"My dinner parties are never dull, even though I am in mourning," said the Dowager reproachfully. "They are merely *respectable.*" She smiled at him mischievously. "I suppose I might depend upon your company any time that I wished, if I could but offer you a selection of opera dancers!"

The Viscount laughed. "I'm afraid not, Mama. I grew past the stage of opera dancers when I was about nineteen. So don't—I beg you—set about organizing a small orgy for my entertainment. I swear you will render me an old man, years before my time!"

The Dowager sighed a little wistfully. "Well, it would not be *entirely* for your benefit, you know. I have frequently wondered what it would be like to participate in an . . . in an *improper* party.''

She saw the look of genuine alarm flash across the Viscount's features, and she sighed. "I dare say I am not wholly serious, Everett. You may put away your scolding expression. It reminds me quite dreadfully of your father in one of his more disagreeable moods.''

The Viscount's lips twitched unwillingly. "Really, Mama! You are incorrigible," he expostulated.

She changed the conversation before he should rebuke her in earnest.

"Everett, I have had another horrid letter from that dismal lawyer, Witherspoon. He told me that the appeal to the High Court had failed, and now Babbington will inherit all your money. Oh Everett! How *could* you let that terrible, depressing Babbington get what is rightfully yours? Whenever Frederick sees me, he stares through those despicable spectacles of his and says, '*Another* new dress, Susannah?' I cannot *bear* to think of him occupying my own dear house in town, and probably tearing out all my beautiful straw silk draperies to replace them with crimson plush! You *know* what abominable taste he has!''

"I think you are worrying unnecessarily, Mama. I cannot believe that my cousin Frederick is at all likely to waste his money on replacing perfectly good curtains, merely because he dislikes the colour. I think you may assume that your silk draperies will be safe for the next generation at least.''

The Dowager looked at him witheringly.

"Why are you talking about curtains? You know quite well that this is not what I meant at all.''

Her face crumpled slightly, and she turned away to hide the faint flush which suffused her cheeks.

"Everett, you are my *son*. I cannot bear to see you throw away your chance for future happiness because of . . . because of . . . Oh! How I *wish* your father had never written that utterly stupid will!''

"Don't we all?" murmured the Viscount. Reluctantly, he stretched out his hands to clasp the Dowager's fingers within his own.

"I have come to tell you something important, my dear. And to ask for your help."

He hesitated, unwilling to confess the truth, but realizing that he could not delay much longer in giving her the news. "I have come to tell you that I am married, Mama. I was married two days ago."

"Oh no!" The Dowager paled. "Oh, Everett! I had hoped, *prayed*, that you would not do it. Think of the people who depend upon you! Think of your father!"

"I must crave your indulgence, ma'am. I never think of my father if it is at all possible to avoid doing so."

"Everett, I cannot believe that she will make you happy." The Dowager's nervous fingers toyed with the elegant silk fringing of her sleeve.

"You know that I would never reproach you for your choice of bride merely because the world might consider her unsuitable. But Lady Angela . . ."

She walked over to her dressing-table in evident agitation, avoiding her son's silent gaze. At last she drew a deep breath and said determinedly.

"I have never thought that Lady Angela Thorpe could make you happy, but I shall do my best to meet her with complaisance since *you* have chosen her."

The Viscount's voice was as cold as his mother had ever heard it.

"In the circumstances, ma'am, I suppose we may count it fortunate that I have not made Lady Angela my bride. You do not know the girl I have married. Her name is Sarah." His lips twisted in an ironic smile. "Sarah Smith until two days ago."

"Sarah *Smith*?" The dowager's voice was blank with astonishment. "But nobody is called Smith, Everett."

"On the contrary, my dear. I believe we can safely say that

it is the commonest name in England."

"You know very well what I mean. You are determined to be disagreeable today. How did you meet her? Who is sponsoring her, for I am sure that there is nobody called Smith whom I can recall. unless . . . is she one of the Lancashire Smiths? I believe I met one of them once. Strange, *northern* sort of people."

"This passion for genealogy is quite new in you, Mama. I thought you had just remarked you would pay no attention to worldly eligibility in my bride. Yet here you are, sounding for all the world like a cross between Jeffries and Witherspoon, about to lecture me upon my responsibilities to the Blackwood name. Are you not going to wish me happy?"

"Oh, but of course. Although I am fully aware of the fact that you haven't answered my questions, you know."

The Viscount found himself once again enfolded in the Dowager's delicately perfumed embrace.

"Tell me about her, Everett. I am so overcome by your news that my wits have flown out of the window. Is she pretty? Shall I like her?"

"I find it difficult to answer your questions. Sarah has been sick. She has never been presented to society—I met her while I was engaged upon a mission of charity."

He observed his mother's astonished expression, and said wryly. "You may recall that my trustees had rebuked me for my frippery behaviour, ma'am. Meeting Sarah was the result of my attempt at character improvement."

He saw that his mother's expression still hovered between disbelief and deep anxiety, and he paced the room restlessly.

"I need your help, Mama. For good or ill, Sarah and I are wed, and for the first time I find myself in agreement with the earnest Mr. Witherspoon. There has been sufficient scandal attached to the Blackwood name. It is time for me to assume some of the burden of administering our estates. I find myself with a wife. I will not attempt to conceal from you that the marriage was a hurried affair, not properly thought out, conducted when I was in my cups. Will you help me see that Sarah does not bring further disgrace upon us? I have already contributed more than my fair share."

"Nonsense!" exclaimed the Dowager roundly. "It is only to be expected that a man will sow a few wild oats before he settles down. If your father had but been prepared to allow nature to take its course . . . But there! It is no use crying over spilt milk. Tell me frankly, why do you expect your wife to cause any scandal? Have you allowed yourself to be thrust into foolishness by one of your fits of temper? When your will is crossed, it is sometimes as if you have the devil himself upon your shoulder."

"If only my father could have remembered that," said the Viscount bitterly. He saw the worry that darkened his mother's face and sat down beside her. "Pay no attention to me, Mama. I will explain to you about Sarah."

He paused, unwilling to reveal to his mother how carelessly he had ventured into marriage, and ashamed that he had relied upon somebody's prospective death to thwart his father's purpose. He could not help seeing the lines of concern that creased the perfection of his mother's forehead, and he noticed the worry that dulled the normal sparkle of the Dowager's eyes. His half-formed desire to protect her from full knowledge of his reckless behaviour, hardened into a firm resolve. It would not be possible to pretend that he had made a brilliant match, but perhaps Sarah could be passed off as the respectable daughter of a country parson. He took his mother's hands between his own, patting them gently.

"Sarah has been neglected by her family, Mama. She is an orphan, and has been brought up by a clergyman and naturally knows nothing of London society. She must regain her strength for a few days, but when she is well, may I rely upon you to ease her path into society? She will need instruction, I am sure, if she is not to become the butt of every malicious gossip-monger in town."

"Well, of course, Everett. You have only to ask." She

sighed a little tremulously. "But how did you come to marry such a girl? Why—when there are so many others who could have served the purpose better?"

The Viscount smiled lightly.

"Now, Mama, you cannot expect me to reveal *all* my secrets at one session! You may whisper to your friends that my marriage sets the seal upon a long and secret romance."

He teased her gently. "You cannot deny that presenting a new daughter-in-law will be much more fun than wondering what to do now that your year of mourning is at an end. In fact, I am beginning to wonder if I did not marry just to please you!"

"At least it puts that odious cousin Frederick in his proper place." The Dowager's expression lightened visibly. "And I may buy myself a new wardrobe."

She tripped over to the wall of mirrors. "Pale lavender with silver trimmings. What do you think, Everett? Would it not be charming—and perfectly proper for a widow?"

The Viscount raised her fingers to his lips.

"I think it would be etnrancing, as you very well know. Will you come and meet Sarah tomorrow morning, Mama? I think she will be strong enough by then. But no wearing her out with difficult questions, mind!"

"You will be unable to keep me away. And since *she* is not an expert at wriggling out of answering questions—not to mention being expert at wrapping me around her little finger—I may just possibly learn something about this mysterious marriage."

The Viscount thought of the pale, determined face lying quiet upon the lacy pillows, and a sudden smile lit up the depths of his eyes.

"It is certainly possible, Mama. But I would not count upon it."

He touched his lips to her slim fingers once again and was gone, leaving the Dowager to watch his progress down the corridor with worried eyes.

Her expression would have been more troubled had she known his destination. It was undoubtedly fortunate, therefore, that the torrid love scene later enacted in Lady Angela's boudoir was, in the nature of things, forever veiled from her view.

SIX

The Viscount knocked at Sarah's door, humming with quiet self-congratulation as he waited for a serving-girl to answer his summons. He strolled into the bedchamber, noting with satisfaction that Dr. Thompson had sent round some respectable old lady to act as a nurse. This woman bobbed a curtsey with becoming humility, smoothing her white apron with capable, toil-worn hands.

The Viscount allowed his gaze to roam around the sick-room, pleased at its orderly appearance. The bedchamber was suffused by the soft light of a blazing fire and several candles. The furniture gleamed with the lustre of fresh polish, and a copper pot, perched on the hob, emitted the fragrance of brewing herbs. He saw four or five bandboxes stacked neatly in one corner, gratifying evidence that his afternoon visit to the Pantheon Bazaar had already born fruit. His wife now possessed a few basic necessities of her own, which ought to satisfy the housekeeper.

The nurse, without being asked, pulled back the draperies surrounding the bed, and curtsied again a little nervously.

"Miss Sarah . . . that is to say, her ladyship, is sleeping, my lord. I don't think it would be wise to waken her up."

The Viscount raised an astonished and supercilious eyebrow.

"She has presumably been sleeping all day, and she may sleep for the rest of the night. But at the moment I wish to talk to her—and in private."

"Yes, m'lord."

The nurse withdrew in defeated silence, avoiding the Viscount's eyes as she scuttled from the room. There was a slight movement from the bed.

"Was it necessary to be so rude to Aggie? She was only trying to protect me."

The Viscount's pleasant mood of self-satisfaction vanished instantly. He stared disbelievingly at the girl in the bed, rather as if he suspected a peg-doll of springing to life while his attention was otherwise engaged.

"I was not aware that you were in need of protection from me. I was rather under the impression—apparently a mistaken one—that you would have been dead had it not been for my intervention. Moreover, I am not in the habit of permitting servants to tell me what I should do."

The grey eyes sparkled with dangerous flashes of fire.

"Aggie is not a servant. She is more of a friend."

"In one day?" The Viscount's voice was derisive. "You are generous in awarding the favour of your friendship."

He was surprised to detect a faint flush that spread along the delicate line of her cheekbones. Her voice was more conciliatory when she spoke again.

"You did say the other night that if I required some service, I had only to ask for it." Her chin rose defiantly. "I asked Dr. Thompson if he could send for Aggie—Agatha Meadows. She was our housekeeper once, and I knew that she would be able to come and nurse me. She has also been caring for Lizzie, the old woman who came here with me from the . . . from the workhouse." The grey eyes were a little pleading. "I thought your servants might appreciate some extra help with two invalids on their hands."

"You are all thoughtfulness," he said sarcastically. "I can see that your recovery has been swifter than any of us anticipated. I had better not stay away from you for two days at a stretch, or I shall return to find the house totally reorganized."

"I should not dream of doing anything so presumptuous, my lord. But it is true that I feel much stronger today. My constitution has always been unfashionably robust."

She stopped speaking and studied the elaborate counterpane on the bed as she struggled to school her voice to suitable humility. "Nevertheless, my lord, I realize that had it not been for your timely intervention, neither my constitution nor anything else could have saved me. The fever ward at that workhouse would have killed off the strongest of mortals, let alone someone who had just spent the night in the river. I am grateful, my lord, but I cannot help wondering how you expect me to demonstrate my thanks. There are very few ways a woman in my situation is able to show her appreciation."

"A little frankness would certainly prove a step in the right direction, madam. You have already told me that you are an orphan, brought up by a kind-hearted minister. You will understand that I find such an autobiography somewhat inadequate for the woman who is now my wife."

The angry sparkle returned to her eyes. "And of course, my lord, *you* have nothing to explain. We all know that Viscounts go into the poorhouse every day in order to select a bride. In fact, one cannot help wondering how all the débutantes of aristocratic lineage ever find suitable husbands, since their menfolk are all out searching the gutters for a bride."

The Viscount strode angrily away from the bed.

"My reasons were adequate, or at least they seemed so at the time. I naturally did not anticipate selecting a sharp-tongued termagant like you for a bride." He laughed harshly. 'I imagined a thief, or a harlot, or even a simple illiterate. I was even foolish enough to imagine that I might receive some gratitude. You will perceive the depth of my error."

"You sound aggrieved, my lord. I am sorry that I failed to conform to your specifications. I regret that I must confess that I have never been either a thief or a harlot. Indeed, except for the fact that my guardian laboured in a parish full of the destitute, I cannot see that my life has been very different from that of many other young women. As a child, I studied and played. As an adult, I kept house for my guardian and learned that the poor have very little time for play." She drew a deep breath and evidently struggled to speak more calmly. "As for my gratitude, my lord, I shall endeavour to display it when once I have regained my strength."

The Viscount ignored this final barb. He seemed occupied in staring at the fire. His expression was hidden in the shadows cast by the great mantelpiece.

"I think we now come once again to my original question, Sarah. If your life was so dull, so full of the normal routines of young womanhood, pray tell me why you were found floating at the edge of the river—and in a state of starvation too."

He looked round quickly, just in time to see the flicker of terror that flashed across her face. It was quickly suppressed, but a faint tremor underscored her words when she spoke again.

"My sister and guardian are both dead. I had no source of income. Why do you find it so hard to accept that I could not find the strength to carry on? Do you have some *reason* for suspecting that my story is untrue?"

"You do not strike me, ma'am, as a woman who is very likely to turn her thoughts to suicide." He looked at her coldly. "I am surprised there was no curate or other worthy gentleman eager to offer you the protection of his name."

"My unc . . . my guardian's parish did not offer us a wide variety of eligible gentlemen, my lord. The curate— you are correct in assuming there was a curate—had been betrothed to my sister Cassie. It is difficult to see how he, a young man struggling to make his way in the Church, could have offered his protection to a young, unmarried woman entirely unrelated to him."

"Ah! So the curate let you down." The Viscount looked at her speculatively, without warmth. "Even so, one disappointment seems unlikely to have driven you to suicide. It does not matter, you know. I shall discover whatever it is you have to hide eventually, and then you may wish you had chosen to confide in me sooner."

She had her feelings well under control again now.

"That is possible, of course, my lord." She looked at him steadily. "What do you plan to do with me, my lord? If you will not tell me why you married me, at least let me know what my future fate is to be."

"You are my wife. You will live the life that befits your station for as long as it pleases me. The estate requires an heir, and since I am married to you, I suppose you will have to provide it. After that, who can say? Your future is secure. Even if I never wish to see you again, I cannot allow it to be said that the Viscountess Blackwood starves in a garret. If you conduct yourself properly, you will be able to occupy yourself caring for the Blackwood heir. Otherwise you will be generously pensioned off, my dear, and the children removed from your undesirable influence."

"You are despicable, my lord," she hissed at him. "And what if I do not agree to your programme?"

"I do not understand your question."

"What if it does not please me to participate in this wild deception? I am no Viscountess. I am not your wife—except by virtue of a strange ceremony conducted when I was half out of my mind with sickness. What if I choose to make public the true facts concerning our manner of meeting, and the absurdity of our wedding ceremony?"

The Viscount's chill voice cut sharply through the mounting hysteria of her questions.

"There are two perfectly good reasons, madam. First, it is not in your own interests to spread such a story. I have rescued you from certain penury and almost certain death. What do you plan to do when once you have spread your rumours? Where will you go? How will you eat? Who will employ you? Secondly, you will do as I say because I *order* you to do it, and I have the power to compel your obedience. I should not shrink from physical violence if I felt it was necessary. Do I make my meaning plain?" -

"Admirably, my lord." Her voice was bitter. "I am a prisoner and your slave, but my bonds will be silken until I displease you."

"Excellent. Your intelligence does you credit, my dear, I am sure we shall contrive to rub along together very agreeably."

He strolled over to the door and placed a languid hand upon the bellrope that would summon her servant.

"By the way, Sarah, My mother, the Dowager Viscountess, plans to visit you tomorrow morning. She believes—or at any rate she hopes—that our marriage is the culmination of a secret attachment that has endured for some weeks. I trust I may rely upon you not to disillusion her preconceptions?"

"Certainly, my lord." She laughed hysterically. "I was unable to resist your pleas for an early marriage because of the strength of my feelings towards you. Is that good enough, my lord?"

The Viscount smiled blandly. "It will do for a start. I am so glad that we are beginning to understand one another, my dear. I hope you sleep well."

"Mama, I would like to present you to Sarah, my wife. I solicit your kindness on her behalf. Sarah, this is my mother, the Dowager Viscountess Blackwood."

The formal words of introduction rolled sonorously around the bed. If Sarah had not already been terrified by the thought of meeting her mother-in-law, such cold formality would certainly have shattered any hope of composure. As it was, she had been lying in bed trembling for the past three hours, and the icy reserve of the Viscount's manner merely increased her natural nervousness to the point of panic. She stared with blank eyes at the awe-inspiring figure in black silk, painfully aware of the inadequacies of her own toilette. The black figure stared back in a silence more awful than the angriest of words.

In fact, the Dowager was silenced through sheer amazement. Well used to her son's taste in women, she had anticipated a bride who was either blonde and bounteously curved or raven-haired and alluring. In her wildest dreams, she had never imagined that Everett might ally himself with a pale, ethereal wraith who looked quite likely to break if breathed upon too heavily.

The Dowager stole one further disbelieving look into the girl's wide grey eyes, and failed to recognize the panic which lurked in their depths. Regally she inclined her head in acknowledgment of the introduction, her mind too confused to think how half-hearted her response must seem to Sarah.

"I must ask you to forgive me for receiving you thus informally," said Sarah unhappily. It seemed obvious that the Dowager was not going to become either a friend or an ally. "Perhaps the Viscount . . . my husband . . . has told you I have been unwell?"

"Sarah contracted a chill which was badly neglected," said the Viscount briskly. "But Dr. Thompson assures me that all danger of complications is now past."

"It was unfortunate that Sarah should have contracted a chill just when you decided to marry her," said the Dowager. "And doubly unfortunate that for some reason it was impossible to make us known to one another before the ceremony."

The Viscount had the grace to look discomfited.

"As you know, Mama, there were good reasons why my marriage could not be delayed. We are fortunate that Sarah felt too weak to resist my pleas for an immediate ceremony. If she had not been sick, I fear I should never have persuaded her to become my wife."

Sarah looked up angrily from her determined study of the pattern on her bedspread. Her nervousness was swallowed up in rage with the Viscount's subtle distortion of the events leading up to their marriage. She threw a fulminating glance of reproach at the Viscount from beneath veiled lashes, and the Dowager was surprised to detect the flash of fire that sparkled in Sarah's cool grey eyes. Curiosity, and a new interest in her painfully pallid daughter-in-law, overcame the Dowager's previous hesitation.

"My dear child," she said softly. "I never thought to be grateful for an attack of fever. But if that was what Everett needed in order to spur him into matrimony, then I must be thankful to the inflammation of the lungs which afflicted you."

"I trust my wife shares your enthusiasm for her sacrifice," remarked the Viscount. His glance dared Sarah to protest the fabric of lies he was weaving so skilfully. "I hope there are no regrets, my love?"

"Indeed not, my lord," Sarah's words were quietly spoken and without malicious inflection, but the dowager sensed the restraint behind the simple sentence. She was suddenly eager to pursue Sarah's acquaintance without her son's interested supervision.

"You may as well go away, Everett." She flashed the Viscount a sweet smile, which made protest almost impossible. "I wish to have a *long* talk with Sarah, and you will only pace about the room like a cat waiting outside a mousehole. Besides, I saw your friend Sir Anthony Browne sitting in the drawing-room. Do you not wish to go and discuss some important topic with him?"

The Viscount looked at her in affectionate exasperation.

"I cannot think of any subject that is more likely to command my attention than the first meeting between my wife and my mother."

"Nonsense," said the Dowager roundly. "If you are with Sir Anthony you may discuss boxing, or a new hunter one of you has just bought. You could even discuss politics. Men are perfectly capable of inventing any number of topics which they are pleased to consider important. I am sure neither your wife nor I could produce anything likely to compete with Gentleman Jim's latest exploit in the ring. Is that not so, my dear?"

The Dowager was surprised to hear a small chuckle from the bed.

"Well, as to that ma'am, I believe the gentleman to whom you refer passed on to a Higher Reward some years ago. It seems most unlikely, therefore, that we could produce conversation sufficiently interesting to compete with anecdotes about his present activities."

The Dowager laughed, pleased to see that her daughter-in-law possessed a sense of humour, and the Viscount lifted his hands in a gesture of resignation.

"I acknowledge defeat. I shall withdraw and leave you both to your conversation. Tony and I may contrive to settle a few problems of state whilst you two mull over the latest fashion in ribbons."

He bowed low over Sarah's hands with false solicitude, leaning closer to whisper in her ear. "Don't *dare* to cause my mother any anxiety."

He straightened up and turned to his mother, his face once again all smiles. "Do not believe all her maidenly disclaimers, Mama. Her feelings towards me are as deep as mine towards her. Is that not right, my love?"

Colour stained the whiteness of Sarah's cheeks. "Deeper and stronger, my lord." Her eyes flashed at him with the now-familiar sparkle. "You have hardly begun to plumb the depths of my feelings towards you."

The Viscount clasped her hand and squeezed it painfully tight. "Such *passion* in your voice, my lady. Desist, or you will shock my mother."

He kissed his mother lightly on her cheek. "I shall return in half an hour to drive you home again, Mama. No, do not bother to protest. I am protecting Sarah—you can see that she is still in need of rest."

The Dowager hardly waited for her son to close the bed-chamber door behind him before walking swiftly across to the bed, where she drew up a small chair and smiled at

Sarah.

"Is Everett exaggerating?" she asked gently. "Must you indeed spend all your days in bed?"

Sarah looked down at the exquisitely jewelled fingers resting lightly on her hand, and a lump came into her throat.

"I find the Viscount a little overwhelming," she confessed at last. "Sometimes I pretend to be more fatigued than I truly am."

"It's perfectly obvious that Everett is never going to tell me how you met," said the Dowager. "Would it be any use if I asked you? I have a reputation for frivolity of mind, my dear, but it does not require a rapier-sharp wit to perceive that you and my son are not the most likely couple to seek one another out."

It was difficult to tell a deliberate lie when the Dowager's kindly voice urged her to confession. Sarah sighed, and wrestled with her conscience. Her natural instinct was to tell the truth, to confess her bewilderment about the whole marriage, to reveal the frightening events of the days preceding her arrival in this house. But caution—the fear instilled by the men who had torn her from her guardian's home and finally thrust her into the river—counselled her to guard her tongue. She still did not know if the Viscount himself was in league with her captors. How could she permit herself to trust his mother? She kept her eyes turned away from the Dowager's friendly scrutiny.

"The Viscount met me in the workhouse administered by the wardens of St. Katharine's parish. My guardian was a minister in one of the poorer sections of the city. Viscount Blackwood was engaged upon some mission of charity at the workhouse."

"My dear child," the Dowager's voice contained a sardonic note painfully reminiscent of the Viscount. "Everett has already regaled me with his own touching version of this story. Do you not feel that you could trust me with the truth? After all, I know my son. He has been my greatest joy and my greatest despair for well over thirty years. He does not visit workhouses, my dear. Neither for charity nor for any other reason."

Sarah pressed herself back against the pillows, as if to draw strength from their padded comfort. The colour ebbed and flowed in her cheeks with feverish intensity.

"I beg you, ma'am, not to press me for answers!" She turned tear-filled eyes towards the Dowager. "Viscount Blackwood met me in St. Katharine's Workhouse, my lady. I swear to you that this is the truth. I have told him that I am not a suitable wife for a man in his position. I promised him that I would pass quietly out of his life. He did not choose to agree with me, ma'am. He can be very . . . forceful . . . in his persuasions, and I allowed him to overrule my objections. But I assure you, ma'am, if I had been stronger, if I had not been so feverish, I would never have allowed him to make such an unequal match. I know it cannot please his friends or his family."

The Dowager patted her arm soothingly. "There, there, you silly child. You must not distress yourself. If we were better acquainted you would know that I am not likely to complain because the match is unequal in terms of fortune. And as far as your birth is concerned, he has assured me it is unexceptional. As a mother, I can only conclude that anybody who could persuade my son into visiting a workhouse, clearly has powers of attraction which I would be foolish to ignore!"

She extracted an elegant wisp of scented lace from one of her pockets, and calmly wiped away the beads of sweat which stood out on Sarah's pale forehead.

"Listen, my dear." The Dowager clasped Sarah's hands between her elegant fingers. "I am chiefly interested in seeing Everett happy, and that is something he hasn't been for many years. Probably not since his younger brother was killed in the Peninsular campaigns, which is an event he still prefers not to mention. If you are the wife of his choice, and if you can make him happy, then I shall not be able to help loving you as my daughter."

"I shall do my very best, ma'am, never to disappoint you." Sarah's voice was husky.

The Dowager gave a small shake of her head. "I declare we have become quite maudlin. Let us talk about clothes, which is a much more rewarding topic. If I am to present you to society as Everett wishes me to do, you must allow me to share in the fun of all your shopping. When do you think you might be well enough to come out with me? Must I be patient for another week? A month?"

Sarah laughed, and for the first time the Dowager heard her voice entirely free of worry. "I will make you a confession, ma'am. I have already been out of bed today." She blushed a trifle self-consciously. "It is sometimes easier to meet a difficult situation if one is an invalid, which is why I retreated again to my bed."

The Dowager attempted to look severe. "I do not think I have ever before been called a difficult situation. However, I am delighted to hear that you are recovering so rapidly from your indisposition, whatever it was." She smiled. "Ah no! Don't look so fearful, my dear. I shall not press you on that point. Only tell me—can we shop this week? I will bring my carriage and two maids. You shall be cosseted, I promise."

An inner amusement lit up the angular planes of Sarah's face. "Such attentions will be a novel experience for me, ma'am, and I shall look forward to our expedition. I feel stronger only to think of it."

The Dowager's soft, perfumed cheek rested briefly against Sarah's pale face. "I think that having a new daughter is going to be very amusing—much more fun than being a widow still in mourning."

Sarah caught her breath. "I hope so, ma'am. I truly hope so!"

SEVEN

Viscount Blackwood was not at all happy to be excluded from the first meetings between his mother and his wife. He was further disgruntled to discover, as he escorted the Dowager back to her house in Portman Square, that a shopping expedition was already agreed upon for the following week. It was not, of course, that he begrudged Sarah the cost of a few gowns. Whatever happened in the future, he now felt obliged to keep the girl clothed, housed and fed. What rankled was the knowledge that Sarah had recovered sufficiently to move from her bed—but had chosen to conceal this information from him.

By the time his valet finished shaving him on Thursday morning, Viscount Blackwood had decided to feel aggrieved. He considered himself a rational man and the trivial irritations of the previous day were not, in themselves, sufficient to overset his good humour. However, during the course of a lonely Wednesday night, he found himself reflecting morosely upon the unsatisfactory nature of his dealings with the woman who was now his wife. He was forced to the disagreeable conclusion that, despite several lengthy conversations and innumerable threats, he actually knew very little more about her than he had done five days previously. She was an orphan, poor, and had been in the care of a minister of the Church. She was also damnably elusive. He had known this the day after their marriage. He knew nothing more almost a week later.

Such a realization did not sit well on the Viscount. He had obliged the girl by removing her from certain death, and this was his reward—an obstinate refusal to behave as the Viscount thought she should. The rage mounted within him and he allowed himself to be dressed without so much as a nod to indicate his continued awareness of the valet's presence. Thomas, after observing the deepening scowl on his master's forehead, was thankful for this sign of forbearance.

In this mood of restless irritation, it was not possible to think of food; so the Viscount's household was treated to the startling sight of the master storming along the hallways to his secretary's room for the second time within a week, and this time without waiting to eat his breakfast. The Viscount walked angrily into the study, wasting no time in the exchange of the usual pleasantries.

"What have you found out about that damned vicar? And what about the girls?"

Mr. Jeffries sprang nervously to his feet. He was very good at writing political speeches (never, to the best of his recollection, actually delivered by Viscount Blackwood) and excellent at administering the details of the vast Blackwood estates. He was not at all comfortable investigating the life histories of obscure personages resident in one of London's more sordid parishes.

"Er . . . I have hired a former member of the Bow Street Runners, my lord. I felt that he would be more in the habit of eliciting the sort of information we require and more accustomed to . . . er . . . the squalor of his surroundings. He tells me only that the Reverend Charles Smith died early in January of the fever rampaging in that part of the city. There was a young woman, a member of his household, who died in December. The people in that parish are very poor, my lord, and not much given to churchgoing. But the Reverend Smith was well thought of in the district, it seems."

"And what of the other young woman? There were two women who assisted him in his parish duties."

"I have no information about her present whereabouts, my lord. She had established a school for some of the girls in the district. It was free, so the mothers in the parish were glad to send their daughters there until they were old enough to work. She didn't keep many pupils once they reached seven or eight, of course. The Runner tells me that she escaped the fever which claimed the life of the Reverend Smith, but she disappeared one night, and nobody's heard tell of her since.''

The Viscount stared moodily at his secretary. Far from being reassured by this confirmation of his wife's own words, he felt himself obscurely troubled. Perturbed by this further evidence of the unsettled state of his own feelings, he chastised himself mentally. What had he hoped for? Proof that his wife was a hardened criminal or a prostitute? The Viscount shook his head angrily.

"Tell the Runner to find out what happened to the other girl. I wish to know when she left the parish and why. I also wish to know when the Reverend Charles Smith arrived to take up his duties in St. Stephens. If he was a man of some education, it seems a strange location to have selected.''

"Yes, sir." Mr. Jeffries fiddled nervously with his newest and best quill, not even noticing when he destroyed its carefully-balanced feathers. "I take it this is a matter of some urgency, sir?''

This guarded question was the nearest he would ever come to asking the Viscount why the investigation was necessary. The Viscount failed to respond to his secretary's unspoken request.

"Yes," he said briefly. "I consider this a matter of extreme urgency.''

He paced back along the hallway, scowled ferociously at a maid unfortunate enough to find herself in his path and suddenly thought of the old nurse he had seen in his wife's sickroom. His brow lightened, and he sat down at the breakfast table in a mood of renewed goodwill. He did not unbend so far as to return the butler's polite greeting, but he did manage to command the nurse's immediate presence without actually barking at the unfortunate footman expected to fulfil his order.

Agatha Meadows presented herself promptly at the Viscount's breakfast table. She curtsied with suitable humility, and the Viscount was again gratified to notice the pleasing cleanliness of her attire and the perfect order of her hair beneath its neat cap. He looked at the woman with false friendliness.

"You have been taking care of Lady Blackwood? I am afraid that I do not recall your name."

"Aggie, my lord." She dropped another curtsey. "I am Agatha Meadows, my lord."

"Well, Aggie, I understand that you have been of service to Lady Blackwood for many years. You must be delighted to come and join her in her new household."

"Yes, my lord."

"It was fortunate she was able to summon you so swiftly. You were in London?"

"Yes, my lord."

The Viscount was annoyed. This conversation was hardly producing the flood of information he had anticipated. Were not all old women supposed to be non-stop gossips? He tried again, a more direct approach this time.

"And how long have you served Lady Blackwood, Aggie? I am sure it must be a long time."

Aggie's eyes looked up from the ground. They were blank and stupid. She twisted her hands nervously.

"Aye, my lord. A good long time."

The Viscount mastered his impatience with difficulty.

"How long, Aggie? How long have you been with Lady Blackwood? When did you join her service and where?"

The servant's expression became increasingly bovine.

"It's a long time, m'lord. I ain't powerful good at numbers. I served the Reverend. It's a long time."

"Did you know Lady Blackwood's parents, Aggie? Come, woman. I am looking for information, and you tell me only that you have served the Reverend for a long time."

The formerly competent nurse seemed to be turning into a

bumbling crone almost in front of the Viscount's eyes. Hesitantly, the woman looked up from her determined study of the patterns in the breakfast-room carpet.

"Miss Sarah and Miss Cassie were orphans, my lord. That's why the Reverend took them in. They was only babies when the Reverend first hired me, my lord. But I never worked for their parents."

"Get out!" The Viscount's outraged bellow echoed down the length of the room and out into the hallway. Agatha Meadows tottered humbly from the room and the Viscount watched her departure with cynical eyes. He was quite certain that he had been treated to a first-class performance by a woman of more-than-average intelligence. He was equally certain that he could question her all morning and she would reveal nothing at all about her mistress or the life she had led in the past. The Viscount realized that he had just encountered one of the more effective defences developed by the labouring classes against the encroachment of their masters. Insolence could be met with retribution. Blank stupidity, while infuriating, presented an impenetrable screen.

The Viscount decided to seek the consolation of his Club, but remembered just in time the recent announcement of his marriage. Having no wish to meet the astonished stares and unbridled curiosity of his peers, he reluctantly abandoned all hope of happiness for the day. He took himself off to Sir Anthony's chambers and there consumed one and a half bottles of his friend's best burgundy without even having the courtesy to comment upon its excellence. Sir Anthony, not normally known as a man of piercing intelligence, was wise enough to ask no questions and to make no comments on his friend's newly-wedded state. They ate a miserable luncheon and talked determinedly of horses.

It was not in the least surprising, therefore, that when the Viscount confronted his wife late in the afternoon, his mood was at its blackest. He was not prepared, he decided sternly, to be deflected by tears or faints or other carefully calculated signs of feminine weakness. His temper was in no way improved when, on striding into his wife's room without the courtesy of a warning knock, he discovered her seated comfortably by the fireside, lost in laughter at some joke shared with a revivified Aggie.

He caught himself up in the act of gnashing his teeth, and managed to control himself sufficiently to speak. Aggie did not wait for his command, but sidled silently out of the room, doing her best to appear invisible. The Viscount towered menacingly over his wife.

"Why did you pretend to be ill when you are not? And has Dr. Thompson given you permission to get out of bed?"

She showed no difficulty in disentangling these contradictory questions. She smiled in a friendly fashion that paid no heed to the Viscount's irate expression or to his angry voice.

"Dr. Thompson tells me that the chill brought on an almost fatal fever. But once the fever broke, he assures me that the danger to my health was in large part finished. He has given me permission to leave my room this evening. Is that not agreeable news?"

"Oh, agreeable news indeed! I suppose now you will be wishing to share my dinner table."

"That would be very pleasant, and would save the servants having to serve dinner in two separate rooms which they might consider somewhat peculiar. Of course, I realize you may have another engagement." She saw the thunderous expression darkening his brow, and smiled gently. "Would you not care to take a seat, my lord? If you are to shout at me, you may as well be comfortable."

"I have no intention of shouting at you, ma'am. It is not my habit to raise my voice to a *lady*." The Viscount resisted the impulse to pace up and down the room, and perched himself on the edge of a chair. "I have come to give you my instructions for the immediate future." He paused and looked at her surreptitiously, but she sat with her head meekly bowed, and her hands folded demurely in her lap.

"Yes. Well. I have decided that I shall escort you into the country, ma'am. I have a small hunting cottage in Leicester-shire, and I shall leave you there with the housekeeper until the end of the season. When I leave London for Wrexham, my family estate, I shall come and fetch you. I hope to introduce you gradually into the society of our neighbour-hood. Perhaps it will be possible to achieve your presen-tation to my friends without too wide a scandal. After all, my mother has agreed to help us."

"I can see that you have thought this through very care-fully, my lord." Sarah's polite words were underlined with secret laughter. "Let me see if I have understood you com-pletely. You wish to introduce me to your world without giving rise to scandalous speculation. Naturally, therefore, you have elected to hurry me out of London at the start of the season—and within the first week of our marriage. Having left me alone and untended for four or five weeks—in a hunting box!!—you plan then to escort me into the heart of a conservative country society. There, still knowing nothing of my character or my natural aptitudes, you will attempt to introduce me, inconspicuously, to your friends. Your fore-thought, my lord, is almost . . . incredible."

"Ah ha!" shouted the Viscount, springing to his feet. "You may make bold to mock me, my girl. But you have mentioned the chief reason for this ridiculous charade. I know nothing of your character, eh? Isn't that what you were pleased to say? And whose fault is that, may I ask? Whose fault is that?"

"Why, I fancy nobody's, my lord. We may lay the blame at the feet of Time. There has scarce been sufficient of that for us to become acquainted with one another."

"Time!" exclaimed the Viscount bitterly. "It is not time but frankness which is lacking, my girl. And well you know it."

A faint uneasiness invaded Sarah's manner, but she

answered tranquilly enough.

"As to that, my lord, I think we have neither one of us been over-anxious to make a full confession. May we not enter into an agreement to allow our past actions to belong to the past? We have the present to share, and the future to worry about. Is that not sufficient?" She flushed slightly, then spoke with renewed constraint. "There is nothing in my past likely to rise up and cause you embarrassment, my lord. You may account for our marriage by any story you care to invent. There will be no awkward skeletons to fall out of the cupboard at a public gathering."

The Viscount failed to feel mollified by his wife's suggestions.

"I see that you have finally realized the potential advantages of your position, ma'am. You wish me to acknowledge you as Viscountess Blackwood and set a public seal of approval on your position as my wife. You haven't taken long to work out how best to ensnare me in your traps, have you, my lady?"

Delicate colour suffused Sarah's cheeks, but her voice remained calm.

"It would be entirely foolish of me to try and pretend that I would prefer to be starving on the dockside rather than resting comfortably in your house, my lord. However, I do not see how you can say that I ensnared you. *You* chose to marry *me*, my lord. I did not entice you into marriage. I was in no fit state to do so."

"So now it is to be all my fault once again!" said the Viscount bitterly. "Very well, ma'am. Since you consider my plans so inadequate, just tell me what plans *you* have concocted for your presentation to society. I have no doubt that you have been scheming busily."

"There was no need to scheme, my lord. The Dowager Viscountess, as you already know, was kind enough to say that she would sponsor my introduction into London society. We plan to go shopping early next week and once I have a wardrobe suitable to my new position, the Dowager has suggested that she will give a large ball. I believe she wishes to mark the end of her period of mourning, and she feels that the introduction of a new daughter-in-law to society would be a suitable excuse."

The Viscount was silent for several minutes, and when he spoke again his manner was calmer, but no less blunt.

"Sarah, my mother is not in possession of all the facts concerning our meeting, as you yourself know. She has only seen you in bed, in circumstances that did not permit her to judge your . . . er . . . your social deportment. She is not aware . . . that is to say . . .Dammit, Sarah, I must needs be frank with you on this point. London society is prepared to suffer eccentric aristocrats, and will even welcome outright fools into its midst providing the fool comes with the proper breeding and background. But London society is occasionally cruel, my dear. It demands certain codes of behaviour, it expects certain social rituals to be observed or you will be rejected out of hand. It is not easy to imitate the manners of the *ton*, Sarah, and I do not know if we could instruct you sufficiently in the few days at our disposal. Do not be offended, my dear. There is no disgrace in having led a humble life. Indeed, your days were probably spent far more usefully helping your guardian than they would have been learning how deeply you should curtsey to a duchess, and how many times you may dance with the same gentleman."

Sarah gave no sign that she was offended by the Viscount's words. She replied evenly, the pleasant tones of her voice unmarred by any note of reproach.

"My guardian came from a long, old-established line of country gentlemen, my lord. It was his sense of duty that caused him to work in London dockyards. His birth would have entitled him to the highest clerical positions in the land. Besides, he was a dear and generous man, and he seemed to feel that he owed my fath . . . Anyway, that is beside the point. My sister and I both attended school in Cheltenham for over three years. In truth, we learned few things there that my guardian could not have taught us better himself. Our teachers, however, were well-trained in one subject. They were bursting with information concerning the niceties of aristocratic living. You may test me, my lord. Every conceivable social grace was thrust upon us. You will not find me lacking in knowledge of etiquette or protocol."

The Viscount found himself loath to hurt her feelings, although he knew that a cheap Dame school of the type she had probably attended would be incapable of providing the knowledge she would need in order to face London's super-cilious society. Partly to humour her, partly to make up for his previous display of temper, he patted her hand in a friendly, though condescending, fashion.

"Very well, my dear. Let us pretend that I am the Prince Regent himself. How would you behave if you were pre-sented to me?"

Sarah rose promptly from her seat. Casting her eyes mod-estly towards the floor, she sank into a deep curtsey. Her left hand held imaginary skirts carefully to one side. Her right hand was held free, waiting for some sign from the "Prince Regent" that would indicate whether or not he wished to touch his own Royal fingers to her hand.

The Viscount was taken aback by the proficiency of her sweeping curtsey. "That is very good, Sarah. I am now Sir Thomas Garrett, who has asked for an introduction to the new Viscountess Blackwood. I am about fifty years old. Show me what you would do."

Sarah dropped a slight curtsey, smiled and said briefly, "How do you do?"

Then she shrugged her shoulders and said, "Can we not stop this game, my lord? There are endless tests you might devise and still not cover all the necessary rules of etiquette. Can you not accept my word for it that I shall not be found lacking? Why should I lie? There would be no point in doing so."

"That is possibly so," said the Viscount slowly. "But then, there seems little reason for you to conceal your past, and yet you do."

"And there seems even less reason for you to lie about your reasons for marrying me." The accusation flashed back from Sarah.

The Viscount's expression was thunderous, but suddenly he laughed. "I will concede the victory to you, Sarah, at least in this round. You are right, after all. What do I have to lose? If you are deliberately outrageous in your behaviour, you will suffer more than I do since I have the power to determine how comfortably you will live. If you make genuine errors, there is some truth in what you said earlier. It matters little whether your social gaffes are committed here or in the country. Either society is equally likely to reject you. And I am entirely likely to become a laughing-stock whatever course I follow."

"What story are you proposing to give out to all your friends, my lord? We must tell the same tale, right from the beginning. I imagine there will be other people—apart from myself—who will be curious to know why you have married me."

The Viscount smiled cynically. "Society is not accustomed to hearing lengthy explanations and apologies from me, Sarah. However, in this instance I am happy to think that we shall be able to tell the truth."

"And what *is* the truth, my lord?"

"Why, it is simple. You were previously dedicated to a life of good works, but during the course of a recent severe illness you relented from your previous obstinate refusal of my suit and agreed to marry me."

Sarah allowed her eyes to travel the considerable length of the Viscount's splendid figure. Her gaze came to rest on the folds of his spotless white neckcloth, embellished with a single blaze of diamonds. She spoke consideringly.

"You do not look very much like a man anxious to press

your suit on a girl dedicated to works of charity, my lord."

The Viscount smiled briefly. "I am relieved to hear it, Sarah." He shrugged his shoulders. "People may think whatever they please. There will be some small amount of talk but what conclusion can society reach which will be harmful to us? The social world must needs have a little scandal to keep itself amused and occupied. I am used to gossip and as for you—you, my dear, will have to learn to hold your head high and to smile a great deal."

She turned her back and spoke into the fireplace. "I shall do my best not to disgrace you, sir."

The Viscount stared at her thin shoulders, and was conscious of a most unusual surge of compassion.

"It would not be easy to bring disgrace upon me, Sarah. My past conduct was such . . . In short, I have to confess that I do not find favour with society's stricter matrons."

She continued to speak to the fire. "You are trying to be kind, sir, but we both know that it is one thing to defy a few conventions and quite another to appear . . . vulgar."

In three strides the Viscount was at her side, forcing her round and searching the depths of her grey eyes.

"Who *are* you?" he demanded harshly. "For the last time, who are you?"

Sarah struggled weakly in his iron grasp. "I was Sarah Jane Smith," she said faintly. "Now I am also your wife."

He flung her from his side, uncaring that she collapsed on to the floor. "It would be well if you could remember that fact, *Lady* Blackwood—and that I intend to be the master in my own house."

The slamming of the bedroom door echoed down the draughty corridors, as Aggie Meadows crept quietly back into her mistress's room. With a frightened cry, she gathered Sarah into her embrace.

"Don't provoke him, Miss Sarah. They say below stairs that he's known for 'is terrible temper."

She restored the silent girl to her chair, tucking a warm

rug around her cold legs and feet. "They also say in the servants' hall that 'e has a mistress, and he's 'ad her for years. A Lady Angela, what was 'oping to marry 'im. Proper chuffed up they are in the kitchen, because 'e chose you. But we know 'e didn't exactly choose you—leastways not in the way his servants are thinking."

"Are you expecting me to ask him to dismiss his mistress, Aggie? Is that the purpose of this conversation?"

Aggie poured hot lemon juice over honey and urged Sarah to drink, conveniently ignoring her charge's sarcastic question.

"Shall I fetch our Jem and ask 'im to make some enquiries, Miss Sarah? Mebbe the Viscount ain't nothing to do with that other lord. Mebbe it's just a coincidence, him wedding you right after the other one tried to 'ave you murdered."

Sarah looked at her servant pityingly. "Maybe he isn't a criminal, Aggie, is that what you think? Then what is he, can you tell me that? A lunatic?" She laughed hysterically. "Which would be your choice for a husband, Aggie? A criminal who is half-inclined to murder you, or a lunatic nobleman who selects his bride from the cesspools of the slums?"

"P'raps he ain't either. Mebbe he's just an 'onest gent who made a mistake."

"Oh yes! Why did I not think of that before? He *thought* he was dancing at Almack's, but actually he was in the workhouse fever ward! It is easy to see how such a confusion occurred!"

Wearily she rested her head against the cushioned back of the chair. "No matter, Aggie. I am tired, that's all. Please do ask your brother to make some enquiries, although what Jem is supposed to ask I cannot think."

"He'll have to go to your mother's relations, Miss Sarah. You should 'ave gone there before, when the Reverend passed away. Now Jem will 'ave to talk to them and find out if *they* can think of any reason why folks would want you out of the way."

"No!" said Sarah sharply. "I'll not have anything to do with that family. They cast my mother aside and refused to acknowledge Cassie's existence, or mine. I will not approach them now, when they rejected my mother's appeals for a reconciliation so many times."

"Jem won't talk to your grandfather direct, not if you don't want it, Miss Sarah. But you 'ave to face facts. You're married to a man and you think he might want to kill you. Don't you think it's time you found out why your mother left 'ome, and why your uncle hid you away in that awful parish?"

"There's no mystery, Aggie, as I've told you before. My mother eloped, which is why she was estranged from her family, and my grandfather did not have a forgiving nature. My uncle was no more and no less than what he seemed: a dedicated man of the Church. He did not precisely hide us away, he simply took us with him when he changed his parish."

Aggie's face assumed the obstinate expression of one who knows she is right.

"Ah ha!" she crowed triumphantly. "So why was this simple parson calling himself Smith, when we both know it ain't his proper name?" She sniffed scornfully. "I knows what I knows, Miss Sarah. And I knows that all your trouble started when that curate who was sweet on Miss Cassie inserted the announcement of her death in the newspapers—and used her proper name. There was two men snooping round the vicarage the very next morning. I should never have left you alone at night, not after I seen those men. I'll never forgive myself for leaving you alone in that neighbourhood. Never."

Sarah hastened to stem the flow of self-recrimination.

"Now Aggie, we have discussed all this before. We had no money. You left me in order to find a job so that I might go back to Cheltenham. I do not consider that searching for employment is dereliction of duty." Her voice was resigned as she gave the old servant's arm a reassuring squeeze. "Very well, Aggie, if it will make you feel better about things, Jem may go to Hampshire and ask some questions. But make sure Jem says nothing to anybody that would reveal my family connections, or where I am to be found now that my uncle is dead. My parents had nothing to do with my mother's family while they lived, and my uncle kept us away from them until the day of his death. I shall never go against my parents' wishes, Aggie."

"All right, dear. That's all right." Aggie's voice was soothing. "You come and have a nice rest now. Jem and Aggie will work it all out, you'll see."

EIGHT

It was not to be expected that Lady Angela Thorpe would lightly accept the loss of Viscount Blackwood. Blessed with a body to rival Venus, the face of an angel, and the soul of a moneylender, Lady Angela had found in the Viscount her perfect mate. He aroused in her a depth of physical passion that no other man could begin to appease. His cynical charm protected her from the terrors of boredom. Moreover, had it not been for the ridiculous provisions of his father's will, the Viscount would have commanded an income sufficient to satisfy even Lady Angela's rapacious heart.

Although the Viscount had never made her a formal offer, Lady Angela justifiably attributed this silence to the Viscount's quaintly old-fashioned sense of honour. The Viscount would not propose marriage until he was absolutely sure the proposal could be carried through. Lady Angela had not been unduly troubled by the omission. She had great faith in the Viscount's powers of organization, and she confidently looked forward to their marriage. She felt sure that the Viscount would contrive some method of protecting his inheritance *and* marrying the woman of his choice. She was careful not to ask herself unpleasant questions such as whether she would still wish to marry the Viscount even without his splendid inheritance. Lady Angela had always been a woman well content to live for the moment, particularly if it happened to be a pleasant moment.

Viscount Blackwood had not revealed to Lady Angela his desperate plans for circumventing the terms of his father's will. This apparent caution was not, in fact, attributable to any lack of trust in his mistress, but rather to some inbred and unnecessary scruple. He found the prospect of a forced marriage and the desire for immediate widowerhood, distasteful in the extreme; and he shied away from telling his chosen bride of the sordid ceremony ahead of him. Had he understood Lady Angela better, he would have felt free to reveal his plans. As it was, she was denied the excitement of watching the Viscount's progress towards becoming a widower. Silenced by his scruples, the Viscount left Lady Angela the night before his marriage proclaiming his undying devotion. When next she saw him, in the company of Sir Anthony and the Honourable Jasper Clarke, he was a married man.

The unfortunate consequences of the Viscount's reticence only became evident when Sarah disobliged her benefactor by refusing to die, and the Viscount was constrained to reveal his marriage to Lady Angela. She was understandably enraged to hear that her lover was now a married man, and the explanation was not made easier by being, perforce, conducted in whispers at a public gathering. The Viscount could not wait for a private assignation and risk Lady Angela hearing the news from an outside source. Lady Angela's temper was scarcely mollified by the Viscount's suggestions that the marriage was a mere formality, entered into solely to comply with the demands of his father's will. The Viscount, in fact, found himself unhappily torn between two previously rigid rules of conduct: the first, that one does not betray the trust of a virtuous lady; the second, that one does not discuss the circumstances of one's marriage with anybody outside the immediate family circle—most especially not with one's mistress.

His dilemma would have been considerably eased had he been able to see Lady Angela as less than a virtuous lady. This insight, which was only too clearly available to his parents and all the females of the *haut ton*, was hidden from the Viscount by Lady Angela's incredible beauty and her skill as an actress. He therefore found himself grappling with yet another unexpected and uncomfortable result of his impetuous marriage. Still torn with longing for Lady Angela, he was loath to ask her to continue as his mistress when there was no longer any prospect of an early marriage.

Lady Angela, whose financial situation did not permit her to dwell overlong on the insulting aspects of Viscount Blackwood's marriage, fortunately solved this problem for him. Quickly recovering from her first flash of rage, she did her best to disabuse him of all unnecessary hesitation. During the course of a long and tempestuous night, in between passionate embraces and murmurs of devotion, Lady Angela managed to convey the message that if she could not be Viscountess Blackwood, she was not averse to remaining a well-paid mistress.

It was on this tolerably happy note that Viscount Blackwood departed from his first post-marital visit to Lady Angela's boudoir. Absorbed during the following two days with his mother, his wife and his efforts to unearth the details of Sarah's past, he was effectively isolated from all contact with London's social world. He had neither time nor energy to reflect upon Lady Angela's position in society once news of his marriage became generally known, nor did he attend any social function which might have thrust awareness of her shattered reputation upon him.

Lady Angela was not similarly isolated. Although she had long ago taken the wise decision not to try for admission to Almack's (thus protecting herself from the ignominy of a cancelled voucher), she did still receive invitations and acknowledgment from most members of the *ton*. In the wake of the Viscount's marriage, however, she began to wonder if all the doors of London society would soon be closed to her. Her affair with the Viscount had been notorious, even scandalous, but society was prepared to forgive much while there still seemed every possibility that her reputation would be redeemed by marriage. Most hostesses were not anxious to slight the future Viscountess Blackwood.

The formal announcement of the Viscount's marriage to

an unknown Miss Sarah Smith immediately took away the only reason that society had continued to countenance Lady Angela's indiscretions. When she ventured out to attend Lady Bishop's musical evening, four days after the Viscount's wedding, she realized the extent of her social ruin. Only the assiduous attentions of several young gentlemen prevented the snubs of the dowagers from becoming painfully apparent.

Lady Angela, an accomplished actress, smiled and laughed, while inside she seethed with the injustice of it all. She waited with mounting impatience for Viscount Blackwood to call and suggest to her some way out of the unhappy situation.

It was Sarah who, all unwittingly, sent the Viscount storming back to Lady Angela's eagerly-waiting arms. In truth, after his first passionate night of reconciliation the Viscount found himself with very little time to spare for thinking about golden hair and soft, rounded bodies. His mind was busily occupied in raging at images of thin shoulders, white cheeks and obstinate chins. When he swept out of Sarah's bedchamber on Wednesday evening, however, a memory of Lady Angela's generous curves rose up to soothe him.

As soon as he discovered that his wife did indeed plan to take dinner downstairs, he sent word to the stables ordering his phaeton. Allowing the butler to assist him into his driving coat, he smiled grimly.

"Please inform Lady Blackwood that I regret I shall be unable to join her at dinner this evening. A prior engagement of a long-standing nature requires that I should be elsewhere."

"Yes, my lord." Potter's blank face suggested that it was entirely natural and proper for the Viscount to depart from his own table on the first evening that his new bride descended to it. The Viscount suppressed an irrational burst of anger, tinged with guilt.

"There is no need to stand there, Potter. You may convey my message to her ladyship."

"Yes, my lord." His retreating back managed to express the shocked disapproval that had been hidden from his face.

The Viscount watched the butler for a minute, then shrugged. He patted his pocket to make sure that he had remembered the velvet box with its diamond bracelet, and schooled his tumultuous thoughts towards the comforts of Lady Angela's bedroom.

Lady Angela, harried by the social failures of the last two days, had prepared herself to express her displeasure in no uncertain terms. Her tears were ready, carefully practised to ensure that their flow did not mar the clear perfection of her china-blue eyes. But the mere sight of the Viscount softened her mood, causing her heart to beat faster under the excitement of his presence. She glowed with triumph that he should visit her so frequently, even though he was now a married man.

They ate dinner in her rooms, and he flattered and charmed her as he always did. She was trembling with passion as he undid her clothes, and there was no pretence at all in her soft moans of pleasure as he carried her to the bed.

Much later, when she was lying drowsy and naked among the cushions, the Viscount said to her tantalizingly, "I have a present for you."

Her eyes widened with immediate anticipation, and her energy returned as he crossed the room and retrieved the flat velvet box from its hiding place. He lifted out the quivering fall of diamonds and wound the spiral of gold and jewels around her wrist, pressing a kiss into the palm of her hand as he closed the clasp. The blue-white fire of the stones shone under the dim lights of the room, and she gasped with pleasure. All thoughts of acrimony or retribution faded once again from her mind. A diamond bracelet could buy a great deal of forgiveness from Lady Angela, especially when accompanied by the Viscount's expert love-making.

She lay back against the pillows, squirming with sensuous beauty into the soft down of the mattress. She tried to listen with half an ear to the Viscount's conversation, but her attention was caught by the entrancing sparkle of light that shimmered from her latest treasure. She sighed, sated and as near to perfect contentment as was possible for a woman of her nature. What did it matter if society looked at her askance? The Viscount was welcome to his nonentity of a wife. *She* was at the centre of his heart and of his thoughts. She fell asleep, still naked, the bracelet pressed close to her heart.

The Viscount adjusted the plain linen of his wristbands beneath the silk of his coat cuffs, and looked at his sleeping mistress. He did not even realize himself how far his thoughts were from the perfumed confines of Lady Angela's bedroom. His eye returned to the golden bracelet. Tomorrow, he decided, he would send Potter to the vault to bring up some of the Blackwood family jewellery. It would be interesting to see the famous sapphires displayed against the slender throat of the new Lady Blackwood.

Lady Angela smiled in her sleep as Viscount Blackwood went softly from the room. For the first time since becoming her lover, he did not stop to drop one last kiss on the gleaming redness of her full lips. He wondered if Sarah was already asleep.

For almost a week after this pleasant encounter with Lady Angela, Viscount Blackwood did not see his wife. His Friday morning tray of chocolate contained a polite, rather uninformative note from his mother, which simply announced that Sarah had already arrived in Mount Street as a guest at the Dowager's house. With his mother's typical vagueness (at least when she wished to avoid uncomfortable explanations) the note hinted that the visit was necessary in order to make shopping quicker and fittings at the dressmaker easier. The Viscount, happy to be relieved of all necessity for seeing Sarah and facing up to the realities of life, returned to his former pursuits with renewed energy.

Five days had gone by before he was forced to concede that "out of sight" was not, in this case, "out of mind". The whole of London seemed intrigued by his marriage, and at least half of London managed to find some excuse for asking him pointed questions about his bride. He soon realized that his deliberately vague hints of a long-standing attachment had grown at the hands of the gossip-mongers into an intriguing tale of a Secret Romance, hitherto hidden from the world. He was fortunately spared knowledge of a second interesting rumour, which suggested that his conquest of Lady Angela had been nothing more than a passing affair, entered into while the course of his True Love ran predictably roughly. Lady Angela, busily buying new outfits to match her ravishing diamond bracelet, was temporarily left in blissful ignorance of this latest attack upon her position.

Viscount Blackwood braved the onslaught of sly questions and continued to turn up at his clubs, and to greet his friends nonchalantly when he tooled his curricle around the Park, or when he strolled down St. James's with Jasper Clarke and Sir Anthony Browne. Inwardly, however, he quailed at the storm he had unleashed over his own head. His friends suffered with him, feeling themselves partly to blame for the disaster they saw looming ahead. After six days of delicate probing, Sir Anthony felt constrained to tackle his friend point blank.

"Look, it's no good beating about the bush, Ev. This thing's gone far enough. What are you going to do when you have to produce Sarah?"

The Viscount was too ill-at-ease to let down his defences, even in the company of his oldest friends.

"I imagine there will be no particular problem. Sarah exists, after all. You sound rather as though you feel she may have disappeared in a puff of smoke."

"Be a good thing if she had," said Jasper with unfortunate

bluntness. "Here's all the old tabbies deciding you're a reformed character—redeemed by the love of a good woman, was what old Lady Avon said to me—and now you're going to have to spring Sarah on them. It won't do, Ev., old fellow. It won't do at all."

The Viscount was absorbed in the contemplation of his snuff box. "You have not seen Lady Balckwood recently, Jasper. I think you may be in for a surprise."

The Honourable Jasper Clarke was astonished to hear Sarah—a chit from the workhouse—referred to as Lady Blackwood. He would have expected the words to stick in the Viscount's haughty throat. Despite this encouraging sign, he was not sufficiently reassured to abandon his worries.

"Fact of it is, old fellow, Tony and I feel responsible. We should have stopped you that night, you know. We were fools to let you go through with it."

"My dear Jasper, pray do not trouble yourself further. I can assure you that I needed no prompting to urge me into folly that day. I think I may confidently assure you that there is nothing you could have done to dissuade me."

Sir Anthony shuffled his feet. "Er . . . we could take her into the country for a while, Everett. My sister's a very good sort of gal and she'd probably . . . well . . . take Sarah in hand a little. Give her some instruction in a few of the basics before she has to come up here and face the music."

The Viscount appeared amused. "I have already been told that such a scheme shows lack of forethought."

"Well, I don't agree, Everett," said Sir Anthony. "Who told you that?"

"Sarah," replied the Viscount briefly.

There was an embarrassed pause, finally broken by Jasper.

"What *are* you planning to do then, Everett? I mean you can't go on for ever saying that your wife's too sick to stir out of doors. Not if you're planning to go on careering around town as if you hadn't a care in the world."

"The matter is quite out of my hands, I assure you. My mother is to introduce her to society by means of a large ball. I have no doubt you will be receiving cards shortly."

If he had hoped to startle his friends, his purpose was achieved in gratifying measure. Sir Anthony and the Honourable Jasper stared at him in stunned silence for several minutes; the latter finally recovered his voice.

"The Dowager Viscountess is giving this ball, Ev? What's she going to say when she meets Sarah?"

"My wife," said the Viscount gently, "has already spent the past six days at my mother's house. Whatever the Dowager Viscountess was planning to say has undoubtedly by now been said. I merely wait to receive my instructions. A mere man is of no account in planning a ball, as I am sure you will fully appreciate."

The others tried to assimilate these new and astonishing pieces of information. They each recalled to mind the wasted figure of a dockside waif whom they had seen wed to the Viscount, and tried to imagine her gracing the table of the Dowager Viscountess. After a short struggle, they abandoned their efforts as ridiculous.

Sir Anthony rose to his feet, casting a last regretful eye in the direction of the Viscount's superlative madeira. Jasper, even more regretfully, followed suit. It was plain that their friend the Viscount was wading into troubled waters and, for reasons they could not understand, he seemed not to care about the perilously shifting sands that lay ahead.

With unspoken accord, they flashed one another conspiratorial glances. The Viscount must be saved from himself before he accomplished his own ruin. They bade the Viscount falsely cheerful good-byes, and sauntered off into the night watched by the cynical and very wide-awake gaze of their host.

His friends genuine concern could not be brushed off as easily as the Viscount would have liked. He tried to turn his mind to other tasks. He read a report submitted by his bailiff and wrote an immediate response that answered all the bailiff's questions so concisely and so specifically that the man was thrown into a frenzy of work for a sennight.

He read a book, newly arrived from France, and currently all the rage among the gentlemen of his acquaintance. It failed—despite some quite astonishing artwork—to stir even a flicker of interest. Surprisingly enough, he did not even think of making the journey to Lady Angela Thorpe's house. Finally, he acknowledged defeat and retreated to his bedchamber, waiting restlessly for the dawn of a new day and the chance to call upon his wife. Hastily he corrected his errant thought. It was his *mother* whom he wished to see, simply because he needed to check on the progress of the arrangements for the Dowager's forthcoming ball. It was a matter of complete indifference to him whether he saw Sarah tomorrow or not. On this very satisfactory thought, the Viscount fell asleep.

NINE

"Everett, my dear, how nice to see you." The Dowager stopped flitting between the billowing piles of silk in her private sitting-room long enough to drop an absent-minded kiss on her son's cheek. The maid plodded patiently behind her mistress, restoring order to the clothes which the Dowager seemed determined to strew around the room. The Viscount smiled indulgently.

"You are looking enchanting, Mama. I see you have finally decided to abandon the black."

"Yes," said the Dowager seriously. "I have been a grieving widow quite long enough. I was monstrously bored with sitting quietly feeling virtuous and mournful." She twirled around with youthful energy. "I think pale mauve is flattering to my complexion, don't you agree?"

"You know very well that your complexion is as close to perfection as it could be, and that you look charming in almost any colour. You are merely looking for compliments, and I am in no mood to humour you today."

The Dowager stopped her twirling and glanced up at him anxiously. "I should have realized something was the matter. You were here only the other day and now you are back again."

"You cut me to the quick, Mama. It is more than a week since I called on you. Haven't you missed me?"

"Well, of course, it's always very pleasant to see you, even if you are not in the best of humours. But now that Sarah is staying with me, I have to confess that time passes so quickly I hardly have time to miss anybody. Are you sure it's a week since you last called? It seems only yesterday."

The Viscount was somewhat disconcerted. "I would not

like you to feel that I was imposing my company upon you too frequently," he said stiffly.

"Oh la! Foolish man. How could you possibly think that? And anyway, I daresay Sarah might be quite pleased to see you. She could tell you what colour coat to wear to the ball." She smiled at him kindly. "So that you do not clash with her gown, my dear. Heavens, Everett, what is the matter with you today? You are looking positively hang-dog, my dear."

"I have several matters to discuss with you, Mama, which are of a personal nature. May I beg for just a few minutes of your undivided attention? If you can tear yourself away from the pile of spangled gauze, that is."

The Dowager spoke briefly to her maid. "You can leave this until later, Mary." She did not wait until the door was closed behind the servant, before she drifted into an elegant pose on the chaise-longue and said sweetly, "Tell me what is on your mind, my love. After all, that is what a mother is for, is it not?"

The Viscount gritted his teeth. "I was not seeking a loving confidante, ma'am. On the contrary, I wanted to find out what absolute nonsense you are up to now."

"Nonsense?" The Dowager looked vague and bewitching, a difficult combination to achieve at any age, but a triumph of art over nature in a woman of fifty. Her voice sounded hurt.

"You surely don't begrudge me the new clothes? Your father was obliging enough to leave me exceptionally well provided for, Everett. I cannot feel that I have to economise just because you are becoming moody." She peered at him anxiously. "You know, sometimes I have the most lowering suspicion that you will turn out to be exactly like your father—all noble rectitude and the terror of the undeserving poor."

The Viscount's thunderous frown lifted and he laughed unwillingly.

"You are a wretched woman, and I know you fear no such destiny for me. With you as a mother, I am quite sure that my noble rectitude will always be very much tempered with an incurable streak of frivolity."

The Dowager appeared only partially reassured. "Well, there is Amelia to think of. Look what happened to her. And than there is Frederick Babbington, who is your father's first cousin, after all. You cannot deny that there is a very depressing streak of sobriety running right through your father's family. Sometimes, when you insist on looking so *earnest*, I cannot help calling poor Amelia to mind."

"My dear ma'am, surely you exaggerate Amelia's sobriety? My sister merely chose to marry a gentleman more interested in country living than in the gaieties of the London season. I cannot see that this certifies Amelia as a woman unalterably opposed to the trivial enjoyments which life offers."

"I suppose not." The Dowager was clearly unconvinced. Her gaze wandered back to the enticing piles of coloured silks, and the Viscount's expression tightened.

"Mama, I am your son, and I have had the privilege of observing you for many years. You are possessed, my dear, of a scheming and devious mind. You know very well that I could not care less if you bought out the entire contents of Madam Whatever-her-name-is' salon. I merely wish to know what you and Sarah are up to, and why it was necessary to remove Sarah from my house with the most inadequate of excuses to explain her departure. I think it is time you let me into the secret, you know. I, after all, am Sarah's husband and I will be the one who has to face the consequences of any social disaster."

The Dowager looked at him with quiet amusement. "I did wonder how long it would be before curiosity got the better of you and you came storming over here to check on Sarah. For a recent bridegroom, you have been somewhat negligent in your attentions, my dear."

"Now that I am here, would it be straining your hospitality too much to ask if I might see my wife?" The Viscount had conveniently forgotten his decision not to seek an interview with Sarah.

The Dowager made no comment, but rang for a footman and despatched him with a message requesting Lady Blackwood's presence.

"I have settled on the 20th for my ball, Everett. March has been such a gloomy month so far that I am sure everybody will be glad of an excuse to come out and forget the miserable weather."

The Viscount had no chance to express his feelings about the desirability of such an imminent date, for their conversation was interrupted by a light tap on the door. Without waiting for permission to enter, a young girl ran gaily into the room, the pale primrose yellow of her skirts flaring out around her. Brown curls clustered in shining coils at her neck, wide grey eyes were alight with laughter.

"What do you think, ma'am? Emmeline has excelled herself with this creation, don't you agree?"

She swept the Dowager a mock curtsey, holding her arms out to display the yellow kid gloves and the artfully draped line of the sleeves. The light from the chandeliers caught the sparkles of gold fire in her hair and gave a creamy glow to her naturally pale skin.

The Viscount caught his breath just in time to prevent a highly unsophisticated gasp escaping from between his lips. Some movement must have betrayed his presence, however, for Sarah whirled round and a swift flush of colour swept over her cheeks.

Her confusion lasted only a second, and then she walked slowly towards the Viscount, her hand held out gracefully.

"My lord." She dipped into a slight curtsey. "It's a pleasure to see you again."

"Sarah . . . You look beautiful!" It was not at all what the Viscount had intended to say. He cleared his throat hastily and inhaled a pinch of snuff with something of his habitual hauteur of manner. "That is to say, the gown is charming. My mother has obviously directed you to an excellent dressmaker. I scarcely recognized you at first."

"It is amazing what the purchase of a costly gown will do for one's appearance," agreed Sarah dryly. "Besides, I was not exactly looking at my best when last we met."

"I've missed you," said the Viscount. "That is to say, I have ... er ... several matters which require discussion. Since it is getting late, I shall join you for luncheon. With your permission, of course, Mama."

The Dowager who had spent her time during the preceding exchange seemingly lost in rapt contemplation of two pairs of evening slippers, now raised vague eyes towards her son.

"Sarah looks so charming, does she not, Everett? It is wonderful how quickly she has pulled back from that depressing chill. I can hardly wait for our ball so that I may have my own back at our odious cousin Frederick. I shall make sure that he knows what an exorbitant sum of money you have been spending on Sarah's clothes. It will be splendid, will it not, to observe him calculating how many Government bonds he could have bought with all the money dancing round the ballroom on Sarah's back!"

"He may refuse the invitation just to spite you, my dear."

"Oh no! Even Cousin Frederick could not possibly be so disagreeable!" The Dowager gave every appearance of one turned into a stone block of misery, but eventually she pulled herself out from this unhappy reverie, and rang the bell for her dresser.

"Did you say that you were staying for dinner, Everett? Or was it merely for luncheon? Sarah and I are going out this afternoon, so I have to get changed. Sarah had better take you away somewhere. You know it makes Mary nervous if people watch her when she is trying to do my hair."

Sarah caught sight of the Viscount's enraged expression

and stifled a giggle. "Dear ma'am, you may leave the Viscount safely in my care. I believe we shall go downstairs and wait for you in the small salon. Perhaps I should ask one of the footmen to fetch up some hock from the cellar?"

"Such an efficient child," said the Dowager happily. "Now do take Everett away. He is making me feel positively haggard this morning!"

The Viscount followed Sarah into a small salon, still fuming at his mother's behaviour. Normally willing to be amused by her deliberate assumption of scatter-brained frivolity, this morning he found himself irked by her skilful evasion of any serious discussion. His tactful questions about Sarah's behaviour not only remained unanswered, they remained unasked. He sat down in front of the blazing fire, ready to take out his ill-humour in a lecture addressed to his wife. He opened his mouth, ready to speak.

"My lord," Sarah smiled at him shyly. "Before you say anything to me, I must take this opportunity to thank you for everything you have done on my behalf. The Dowager Viscountess has been kindness itself to me, and I do not believe I have ever in my life spent six such entirely happy days." A small laugh trembled irresistibly on her lips. "My . . . guardian would have been dismayed to see what happened to my well-trained mind after only two or three hours in your mother's company. I find that I have a natural talent for spending a great deal of time pondering such weighty questions as whether it would be better to choose yellow silk with brown velvet trimmings, or brown velvet with yellow silk trimmings! Last week, when I was in your house, I was at first too sick and then later too worried to express my thanks adequately."

She drew a deep breath. "Whatever your motives in marrying me, my lord, I have decided it is high time to express my gratitude. I should be a fool if I tried to pretend that my old life was anywhere near as pleasant as my new."

The Viscount, who had approached the salon mentally armed with a long list of complaints and instructions he wished to impart to his wife, found himself unable to recall any of them to mind. Instead, he smiled at her with a natural warmth she had never before seen.

"You obviously considered it a matter of some urgency to get rid of that lengthy speech. Why, I wonder?

She looked somewhat self-conscious. "It was because of my temper, my lord. I am afraid that I suffer from what my sister Cassie called a 'volatile temperament'. I had to speak right away, in case you said something to make me fly off into one of my rages. Now that I have thanked you, I consider I have discharged my conscience, so you may feel quite at liberty to provoke me if you wish to do so."

"That is indeed a tempting offer! However, I wish to discuss nothing more harassing than your plans for the ball. My mother tells me that I must know the colour of your gown so that I do not spoil everything by arriving in clothes that clash with your own. Am I to be trusted with the secret of what you will be wearing?"

"Only if you are prepared to make a personal visit to Madame Emmeline's salon, my lord. Otherwise you will have to make do with hearing that my gown is of an unusual colour, somewhere between blue and green."

"Heaven forbid that I should attempt to brave Madame Emmeline's exclusive portals. It would undoubtedly cause her to add at least another twenty guineas to her bill! I shall bear in mind that you will be looking ravishing in turquoise, and select my own ensemble accordingly. For the first dance, you and I will be expected to head the set. Are you sure—forgive me for asking this once again—are you sure that you are familiar with all the steps and movements?"

"Very familiar, my lord." Her eyes were demurely lowered, but a thread of laughter ran through her voice.

"While we were still at school I had high hopes of persuading the dancing master to marry me, so I was a most attentive pupil. Mr. Davenport seemed quite willing to fall in with my schemes, but the headmistress unfortunately disagreed with him. The wretched man was dismissed before we had had much opportunity to exchange more than languishing looks, and I was left nursing a broken heart. At the time, I thought it very poor-spirited of Mr Davenport and quite odious of the headmistress. Then I discovered that he already had a wife and seven children. It was my first bitter lesson in the devious stratagems of men who are pursuing innocent females. Unfortunately, instead of turning my interest to nobler matters, it merely inspired in me a stern resolve to make a wiser selection next time I fell in love."

The Viscount was amused. "And did you?"

Sarah shrugged. "We finished school soon after that, my lord, and left such childish flirtations behind us." She laughed lightly, deliberately brushing aside the slight note of depression. "There were no amatory adventures after the dancing master until my encounter with you, my lord. I would not say that my marriage proves I have perfected my selection process!"

"But you have hardly given me a chance to prove my undoubted moral superiority to the dancing master," said the Viscount. "At least I have no other wife hidden in the background, which must surely be accounted in my favour." He stood up and crossed to her side, pulling her gently into his arms. He placed his hand firmly beneath her chin, forcing her to turn her eyes up to his face. He, in turn, looked down silently at the perfection of her creamy complexion and the unreadable expression in the depths of her dark grey eyes.

"I cannot believe that the dancing master is going to provide me with serious competition," he murmured and bent his head to brush her lips with his own.

Her body stiffened in his arms, and she made to move

away, but he held her more closely, startled by his own impatient desire to embrace her more passionately. His mouth descended again to kiss her with real passion, and he felt her lips soften. When he heard the door open behind them, he felt a flash of angry frustration, which he swiftly masked as his mother came into the room.

The Viscount moved away from Sarah's side. He was not sure if he was more embarrassed to have been discovered making love to his own wife, or angry at having been interrupted. He stole a covert glance at Sarah. She, he was irked to discover, looked perfectly composed. Only an attractive trace of pink along her high cheekbones suggested she was perhaps less tranquil inside than she appeared on the surface.

The Dowager was tactful enough to make no reference to the scene she had just interrupted. She drifted over to the fire with her usual grace, and sank on to a convenient chair in a soft flurry of pale mauve silk. A footman, trailing in her wake, provided them all with refreshments. The Dowager smiled sweetly at Sarah.

"My love, would you be an angel and find the list we made of guests for the ball? I think we should give it to Everett, so that he may add the names of any of his friends whom we may have forgotten. Since this is to be your formal introduction to the *ton*, we do not wish to overlook anybody who may be helpful in seeing you firmly established. Do you remember where I put it?"

"It is in the escritoire in the library," said Sarah. "I will fetch it at once."

"Such a dear girl," murmured the Dowager as Sarah left the room. She continued in exactly the same tone of voice, "I have, of course, invited Lady Angela Thorpe to the ball."

The Viscount was horrified. "Have you taken leave of your senses, Mama? How could you offer such an insult to . . ." He was about to say "Lady Angela" when it struck him with sudden force that the insult to Sarah was even greater. He was forced to subside into irresolute silence.

The Dowager was unperturbed. "I believe, Everett, although mothers are supposed to pretend that they know nothing at all about their sons' love affairs, that we had better deal with this matter frankly. I know, your father knew, and—I am forced to conclude—all the world knows, that Lady Angela is your mistress. *She* has not an ounce of discretion in her delightfully rounded body and *you* seem perfectly content to provide society with a fresh scandal every week. I have had at least three friends who could not wait to pay me a morning call in order to impart the news that my son had been seen entering Lady Angela's house at least twice in the first week of his marriage."

The Viscount interrupted her with a small exclamation of distaste. "I regret that you have been placed in an uncomfortable position, Ma'am, but it is not my habit to adjust my conduct to suit the pleasures of every scandal-monger who cares to poke his nose into my affairs."

"Your behaviour with Lady Angela in the past is naturally something I would not presume to comment upon," said the Dowager gently. "But I have chosen to sponsor the introduction of your wife into society, and I intend to see that her passage is a smooth one. For her own sake, my dear, as well as for yours."

The Dowager looked at her son with considering eyes. "I would in any event have tried to like the wife of your choice, Everett. But with Sarah, there is no effort involved. I do not think you have as yet appreciated the good fortune which caused you to select Sarah as your bride. Anyway, that is all beside the point. I shall acknowledge Lady Angela by inviting her to my party. I wish to put to rest, Everett, any gossip which would try to suggest you have married a nonentity merely so that you may continue to devote all your time to your mistress. Lady Angela will be here at the ball, and allowed to suffer no particular snubs from my friends. But she will receive *no* special attention from anybody. It will be seen that her public rôle in your life is over—quite finished." She sipped absently at her glass of champagne, then smiled at her son. "What arrangement you care to make with her privately is, of course, no concern of mine at all."

"Well, I am certainly relieved to hear that! When you said that you intended to speak frankly you were not mincing matters, I see."

"Sometimes it is better to speak clearly at the outset," said the Dowager tranquilly. "You would do well to remember that in your dealings with Sarah. It saves so much confusion and wasted energy in the end. And here is Sarah, returning with the list. Come Everett, you shall give us your opinion as to whether we have selected our guests well. I sent word of your marriage to Amelia last week and would you believe that George replied with an *express* to tell us they are both posting up for the ball! I did not know that George ever got out of his hunting jacket at this time of year!"

The Viscount smiled at Sarah. "Now you may begin to suspect the extent of your social power. For once my mother doesn't exaggerate. I have never before known George to set foot in town during March—and to commit himself quite willingly it seems! We had better hasten to import dancers from China at the very least, otherwise he will consider the whole trip sadly wasted."

"Nonsense," said the Dowager roundly. "Sarah will undoubtedly captivate his heart."

"If you are both trying to make me nervous of this coming ordeal, you are certainly succeeding!" Sarah's reply was only partially jesting. "How can I hope to live up to such expectations?"

The butler entered the salon to announce that luncheon was served.

"And that is a most fortunate interruption," remarked the Viscount, offering an arm to each of the ladies. "By the time you have eaten, Sarah, your courage will be quite returned. I cannot believe that a mere ball—even one graced with my sister's presence—is going to alarm you in the slightest."

"You place too great a reliance upon my natural fortitude, my lord."

Courteously he led her to her chair at the massive dining-table.

"I think not, Sarah. I really think not."

TEN

The Dowager Viscountess, whose vague manner disguised an excellent capacity for organization, had never in the past felt any need to worry about the preparations for a party. Having lived for more than fifty years as a pampered daughter and wife, it never seriously crossed her mind that her wishes, once expressed, would not be deferred to. Despite noting the harassed wrinkles which occasionally crossed her daughter-in-law's brow, it therefore did not occur to the dowager that Sarah, brought up in a household almost devoid of servants, was living through the days prior to the ball in an agony of suppressed trepidation.

The Dowager Viscountess confidently made her plans for Sarah's début in much the same way she had organized every other gala occasion during her long career as a premier society hostess. She first told the butler to arrange delivery of the invitation cards (written out in Sarah's neat, copperplate hand). She then selected the potted palms which were to grace the conservatory and instructed the servants to decorate the ballroom with gold and yellow satin ribbons. "So springlike!" she murmured happily to an agitated Sarah. She despatched a footman to notify her favourite musicians that they were required to attend on the evening of the twentieth, and she conferred at length with her chef. She even remembered to send round to the stables and arrange for straw to be laid over the paving stones, thus quietening the noise of arriving and departing carriages. As far as the Dowager Viscountess was concerned, her share in the preparations was then complete, and she spent the days leading up to the ball untroubled by any desire to supervise the implementation of her various instructions. Such mundane considerations as the laundering of special linens, the washing of crystal and china, the polishing of silver, and the instructions to the caterers, never once disturbed the tranquillity of her mind.

On the day of the ball, she retired to her bedchamber immediately after lunch, for, as she confided charmingly to Sarah, she could not bear to have her guests whispering that she had turned into a crumpled old hag now that she was a widow.

Sarah was happy to be able to reassure her. On this point, at least, there was no need for false cheerfulness.

"Anybody less like an old hag, ma'am, it would be hard to imagine."

The Dowager smiled gratefully. "You are a dear child, and you lie most graciously." She gave Sarah an anxious inspection. "But you are a trifle pale, my dear. You look worried about something. I trust I have not been overworking you?"

"How can you suggest such a thing? We have done nothing but amuse ourselves for more than two weeks now."

"I have allowed myself to forget, however, that less than a month ago you were dangerously ill. You must rest today, Sarah. Go to bed this afternoon. I am determined that you shall bewitch all our guests!" A small smile hovered on the Dowager's lips. "And Everett, of course."

Sarah turned away, so that her expression was hidden.

"I do not think that the Viscount is very easily bewitched, ma'am. I should . . . I should prefer to keep active this afternoon. I am not really sleepy."

The Dowager did not press her advice, but went contentedly to her room and there slept untroubled by any visions of possible disaster. Sarah, who was not blessed with the Dowager's sublime faith in the satisfactory progress of the preparations, had the greatest difficulty in preventing herself fluttering around the men erecting the awnings, the footmen cleaning the lustres of the chandeliers, and the army of servants dusting and polishing every available surface. When finally she collided with a small maid scurrying submerged behind a pile of white damask napkins—thus scattering eight dozen pieces of clean linen all over the hall floor—Agatha Meadows was sent out from the servants' quarters to have a tactful word with her mistress.

Thereafter, Sarah was reduced to walking up and down the Dowager's private sitting-room, prey first to the mournful conviction that the Viscount would forget to attend his own wife's début, and then to the even more lowering reflection that she would probably make such a mull of the whole affair that, even if the Viscount came, he would be forced to disown her. She wondered how she could ever have been so foolish as to claim to the Viscount that the London season held no terrors for her. It was a decided relief when dusk finally descended upon the streets of the city, and she knew it was time to go upstairs and change into her clothes for the ball.

The Honourable Lady Amelia Sutton and her husband, Sir George Sutton, Baronet, no longer participated in the joys of the London season. Sir George, a worthy landlord and kindly father of six children, found himself well occupied in tending his lands and seeing that the affairs of the county proceeded in a manner suited to his notion of what was right and proper. The labourers on Sir George's lands were expected to work hard during fine weather, but in return he tided them over the dead months of winter when there was no work, and saw to it that their children were clothed and fed when illness struck the breadwinner.

Lady Amelia, who had once justifiably considered herself a somewhat glittering star on London's social horizon, had fallen in love with Sir George's stolid kindness during her first season, and now seemed well content with her rôle as the producer of endless little Suttons, all as plump and cheerful as their father.

The Dowager, who did not find this bucolic idyll of marital bliss altogether to her taste, cast suspicious glances in the direction of Amelia's waistline. She was relieved to see that it remained remarkably trim for the mother of six children, and gave no hint that the Sutton progeny was about to be increased.

Lady Amelia caught her mother's look, and grinned mischievously as she kissed the Dowager's satin-smooth cheek. "Mama, you are looking charming. Most unmatronly. And you will be delighted to learn that I am *not* about to present Sir George with my seventh pledge of affection!" Her eyes twinkled up at the imperturbable Sir George. "On the contrary, we have decided that he is to present me with a token of *his* affection, and I am to refurbish my wardrobe at an establishment which has a little more to offer than the dressmaker in Margate! I am delighted that Everett has finally decided to take the plunge into matrimony. It provided me with the final spur which I needed to roust George from the saddle and into the travelling carriage."

"I am so glad that you both decided to come up to town," said the Dowager. "I know how much you will enjoy meeting Sarah. I trust you were not fatigued by the journey yesterday? And that you find your sister well. Sir George?"

"Yes to both questions, ma'am. She only regrets that her imminent confinement prevents her being here tonight."

"I suppose we may count it miracle enough that Amelia was able to attend," remarked the Dowager with some asperity. The footman finished unwinding Lady Amelia from her fur wraps, and the Dowager looked at her affectionately.

"I must say, Amelia, that for somebody who is buried in the wilds of the countryside and has six children besides, you are not looking at all bad."

Sir George smiled placidly. "But that, ma'am, is only to be expected. She is your daughter, after all."

The Dowager looked at her son-in-law appreciatively.

"I have always felt you were quite *wasted* down in Kent, Sir George! Do you know there are some men who simply never learn how to pay a compliment, even after years of practice? But you have always known how to do it, right from the start."

"I needed a ready tongue, ma'am, as well as a calm disposition. How else was a simple countryman such as myself to persuade a dashing town beauty to be my wife?"

"Dear George!" Lady Amelia sighed happily. "As if you ever thought the issue to be in doubt. One of the most endearing qualities of English country gentlemen is their incapacity to see more than one point of view. George simply decided that I should marry him. After that, no possibility of failure ever crossed his mind." Without waiting to draw breath she turned eagerly to her mother.

"But now, Mama, you must tell me *all*, quickly before the other guests arrive. I wish we had had time to call on you yesterday, but we arrived at George's sister late, and now there is scarcely any time for a gossip! Whatever persuaded Everett to marry right at the last moment, when we had all quite decided he was going to allow Cousin Frederick to inherit? And what is his wife like? Does she know about Lady Angela?"

It was at this inauspicious moment that Sarah chose to enter the drawing-room. Nervous of the ordeal ahead, and preoccupied with questions about her own appearance, she heard Lady Amelia's words without absorbing their meaning. She could see all too plainly, however, the embarrassment written on all three of the faces which turned to observe her entrance.

She faltered at the threshold of the drawing-room, a delicate flush creeping up the normal ivory pallor of her skin. Self-consciously, her hand gestured to the pale turquoise tulle of her gown, and the deeper sea-green silk of the underslip.

"I'm sorry," she said breathlessly. "Have I chosen the

wrong dress?" She looked anxiously at the Dowager. "I could change into the cream crêpe if you thought it more suitable."

The Dowager rose to her feet and made a move to welcome Sarah to her side.

"You cannot possibly be serious, my dear! You are enchanting in that colour." Her swift gaze took in the coronet of fresh flowers woven into Sarah's luxuriant fall of golden-brown curls, and the single strand of gold twisted around her slim wrist. She said nothing about the conspicuous absence of jewellery, although she was furious that Everett had neglected to attend to this essential task. At least, she thought silently, if ever anybody could carry off such a simplicity of fashion, Sarah would be that person.

"Everything is perfect, my dear." She smiled warmly. "You cannot fail to capture at least a dozen hearts! Come over here and let me introduce your new sister-in-law to you. But I must first beg you not to flirt with Sir George. He has six children back home in Kent, and he has no time to spare trying to capture your favours!"

Sarah laughed shyly and came into the centre of the room. "Lady Amelia?" She dropped a small curtsey. "I am so very happy that you were able to come up to town. The Dowager Viscountess told me that you are not often able to leave the responsibilities you have in Kent."

Lady Amelia laughed good-naturedly. "I'll wager that Mama said nothing so tactful! My dear, we have always said that Everett was born under the care of at least three different guardian angels, but in this instance he has outdone himself! Wherever did he meet you? You're so beautiful, and hardly old enough to be out of the schoolroom."

"Appearances are deceptive, Lady Amelia. I am more than nineteen."

"Well, well," said Sir George, bowing over her hand with avuncular charm. "That is certainly a great age. You will have to make allowances for poor Amelia and me. When you have reached the advanced ages of three-and-forty and two-and-thirty, it is easy to forget that nineteen can seem a very respectable accumulation of years. And it's not a bit of good looking daggers at me, Amelia. Your mother and I both know quite well that you were two-and-thirty four months ago."

He smiled cheerfully at Sarah. "Her eldest son will shortly be fifteen, and she wishes me to tell the world that she is five-and-twenty. If only her arithmetic were a trifle better, even she would see the difficulties in that!"

Sarah looked solemnly at Lady Amelia. "My arithmetic was always appalling—quite the despair of my guardian. I cannot imagine why anybody should need to know that you are a day over five-and-twenty."

"Do not listen to my wife, Amelia. She has a charming tongue and I can assure you she will wheedle you out of your last sixpence if you let her." Viscount Blackwood strolled casually into the room, bowing politely to Sir George and bestowing a brotherly peck on Lady Amelia's cheek. He raised his mother's hands to his lips and smiled at her benignly.

"Well, Mama, I hope you are feeling matriarchal. We need only to gather Sir George's brood of little Suttons around us, and we could pose for a family portrait that would rival King George."

"Even with my six, we are still missing several children," responded Lady Amelia somewhat tartly. "You and Sarah must contribute five more before we can compete with the Royal Family."

The Viscount turned a laughing eye in Sarah's direction, but she would not meet his gaze.

"Well, Sarah?" he said mockingly. "Are we prepared to accept the challenge?"

"I cannot plan so far ahead, my lord," she said evenly. "At the moment I feel it would be enough if I can survive this ball."

The entrance of Lord and Lady Frederick Babbington precluded the possibility of further conversation. Sarah, whose knowledge of Lord Babbington sprang solely from the Dowager's slanderous descriptions, was hard put to reconcile the mild-mannered actuality with the scheming miser of her mother-in-law's highly-spiced conversations. Lady Babbington, a stout matron of indeterminate years, was shabbily draped in a gown of virulent maroon velvet. After two small glasses of madeira, it was seen that Lady Babbington had chosen this colour carefully, since it precisely matched the heightened purple of her own cheeks.

Sarah, having made this unfortunate mental observation, was forced to stuff the back of her hand into her mouth in order to stifle a gasp of laughter. She looked up to find the Viscount's disconcertingly alert gaze riveted upon her. He came across to her side.

"Your dress is perfect," he said abruptly. "You should have asked me to bring you some jewellery. I have already sent the family sapphires out to be cleaned. We must go over the rest of the collection so that you may tell me what you might like to wear."

"Oh no! That is not necessary, my lord." She stirred uncomfortably under the continued intensity of his look.

"It is necessary because I say it is," he said finally. His eyes fell as if hypnotized by the slender column of her neck. "Although it is hard to see how your appearance could be improved by the addition of mere jewels."

Some of Sarah's natural poise was beginning to return.

"My lord," she said. "I think the Dowager should have warned me that you are an accomplished and shameless flirt."

He looked at her enquiringly. "What does that remark mean precisely?"

"Your mother has been good enough to provide me with a list of names to remember. I have learned who is of political importance—and whether they are Whig or Tory, of course!

I know all the gazetted fortune hunters. I know all the matrons whom I must impress with my impeccable propriety. And I was also warned about the incorrigible flirts. However, I believe your mother's partiality has blinded her to the one name which should be at the head of that list!"

The Viscount shook his head slowly. "You are quite wrong. When one flirts, by definition one's intentions are not serious. I am not flirting, Sarah. Not with you."

"For shame!" she said lightly, although her voice was a little breathless. "How am I to improve my party skills, if my own husband will not indulge me by playing the game?"

"I do not think your skills require any improvement, Sarah. I suspect that you were bewitching your menfolk whilst you were still in the cradle."

"Not in the cradle, my lord. But perhaps in the nursery. It was well-known in our household that the baker's boy always slipped in an extra jam-tart especially for me."

The Viscount laughed. "You are a shameless hussy and I knew it from the first. Do not expect me to be drawn into your toils, however. Do not let your success with the baker's boy run to your head."

"There is always the sad episode with the dancing master to keep me from becoming entirely puffed-up with notions of my own attractions."

"Very true. I have reason to be grateful to the dancing master." He drew her hand through his arm. "My mother's brother has just arrived. He is a member of our government and a very important fellow. Or at least, that is what he tells us all. Let me go and make him known to you, then we may all go into dinner. I have several more cousins scattered around the countryside, but this small group represents the closest members of my family." His eyes glanced down at her. "It was thoughtful of my mother to make sure that you would meet the family before the start of the ball. At least there will be some familiar faces for you to turn to."

"Six among two hundred!" Her mouth twisted in a rueful

smile. "I am not sure that it will suffice to make me *entirely* at my ease!"

"Oh! I am not worried. Society loves an unknown beauty, my dear, and you fulfil both requirements to perfection. Come! Let us hurry and make the introductions. I can see that Uncle William is looking hungry, so we must catch his attention before it is quite lost among the jellied prawns."

It was not afterwards possible to determine the precise moment at which society decided that the Dowager Viscountess Blackwood's ball should be accounted a success. There was no agreed formula for deciding which function would receive the seal of social approval and which would not. However, even before Viscount Blackwood led his new wife out on to the floor in order to open the dancing, it was clear that London had agreed to be charmed.

Sarah, pale and slim, but smiling with apparent serenity, moved through the complicated figures of the dance with an ethereal grace that set her quite apart from the fashionably buxom beauties. The Viscount, although his expression remained as inscrutable as ever, was seen to keep his eyes riveted on the figure of his bride, and to smile at her with unusual warmth when the set was over. Society, prepared for once to believe its own tales of romance, concluded that this was indeed a love-match.

The Dowager Viscountess, sitting next to her brother and watching the dancing with outward tranquillity, covertly examined the expression of her guests and allowed a small sigh of relief to escape her lips. Her brother, Sir William Haversham, patted her kindly upon the arm. Beneath a pompous and crusty exterior, he nurtured a decided soft spot for his flighty sister.

"Beautiful gal, eh? You must be very pleased, m'dear. I'll tell you frankly, we all feared the worst right up until last month. Terrible thing if Babbington had inherited the estate. The fellow's not up to it. And as for his wife!" His eye caught a flash of golden curls bouncing down the set of dancers. "What the devil . . . Sorry, m'dear. What on earth is Lady Thorpe doing here? I hoped that nonsense was all over."

"But of course," replied the Dowager with a confidence she was far from feeling. "It is because it's all over that Lady Angela Thorpe is here."

She caught the attention of a passing guest, and turned to him with some relief.

"Jasper Clarke! Everett told me that you were a witness at his wedding." She tapped him reproachfully on the arm with her fan. "La, sir! I thought you my friend. How could you permit the Viscount to wed without allowing me to share in the festivities?"

The Honourable Jasper Clarke, who was still reeling under the shock of discovering his dockside waif transformed into a woman of evident culture and stunning beauty, looked warily at his hostess. He was not noted for nimbleness of thought.

"Lady Blackwood was sick," he managed at last. "There were no festivities. Grave fears for her life. Yes, that's it. Ev. was afraid that she might not last the night. Anxious to tie the knot before it was all over."

"Was he indeed?" The Dowager Viscountess seemed well pleased with this response. "So *that* was his plan." She turned a beaming smile on the disconsolate Jasper, who was uncomfortably aware of having betrayed more than he intended, without being at all sure how this had happened.

"Er . . . magnificent party," he said in an effort to change the subject. "Lady Blackwood looking delightful. And you too, of course."

"Thank you, Jasper," said the Dowager with complete sincerity. "I know that praise from you is praise worth receiving. Now, will you forgive me if I leave you to see what is happening in the card room?"

She moved away in a perfumed cloud of silk, leaving him

drooping somewhat uncomfortably at the edge of the dance floor. He wished he could find Sir Anthony, who seemed temporarily to have disappeared. This whole affair was rendering him decidingly nervous. His reverie was disturbed not by Sir Anthony, but by the Viscount himself, who came up and addressed him quizzingly.

"You are looking unnecessarily gloomy, Jasper. Do you not find Lady Blackwood's health marvellously improved?"

"Not only her health," said his friend impulsively. "She looks absolutely stunning, Everett. How did you do it?"

"My dear Jasper, I have done nothing other than to provide a place where she could rest and partake of some nourishing food. Nature has performed the remainder of the miracle."

Jasper was longing to ask how a girl from the slums—even admitting the full wonders of Nature—could be transformed within the space of a few weeks into a lady of the first rank of elegance. Some half-glimpsed barrier in the Viscount's manner almost prevented his broaching the subject, but curiosity overwhelmed him. The Viscount was, after all, one of his oldest friends.

"How did such a girl end up in the workhouse, Everett?" he blurted out.

"I have no intention of telling you at this precise moment, Jasper, so I beg you not to grasp my arm *quite* so violently. My sleeve seems unlikely to recover from your attack upon it."

The young man shrugged in rueful resignation. He knew the Viscount too well in this sort of mood, and accepted that there was no point in trying to pursue his questions. Unoffended, he grinned and clapped his friend on the arm.

"I rely upon you to procure me the first waltz! Tony and I must be her oldest acquaintances in the room, after all. And you know Tony will be at the gaming tables until after midnight, so my claim stands higher than any other."

"I will do my best on your behalf." A small smile hovered

around the Viscount's lips. "I would not say that my word always carried the weight with Sarah which one might hope for. She does not seem to suffer from an excessive sense of obligation. On the contrary, she seems to harbour some resentment for my arbitrary decision to marry her. Perhaps it would be better not to remind her that you participated in her selection from the . . . er . . . the place where we met."

He led a puzzled Jasper across the ballroom. They found Sarah seated next to Lady Amelia Sutton and surrounded by an eager coterie of young men. She looked up at their approach, sensing the Viscount's presence before he spoke. A smile of dazzling beauty lit up her face, giving colour to her cheeks and deepening the smoky grey of her eyes. Jasper happened to glance up at his friend at the moment Sarah smiled, and he witnessed a fleeting flicker of emotion such as he had never thought to see written upon the Viscount's cynical features.

For the first time, he felt a strong personal interest in the girl whom they had found dying in St. Katherine's fever ward, and he pressed forward, eager for his dance. He admitted to himself that he was curious to see what manner of woman could cause the Viscount to smile so tenderly.

And what of Lady Angela Thorpe? In common with the rest of the Dowager's guests—not to mention the Dowager—he was looking forward with thinly-concealed interest to the moment when the two notorious lovers finally danced together. Altogether, he thought, this promised to be a fascinating evening.

ELEVEN

If Sarah and her mother-in-law were, on the whole, well pleased with the progress of the ball, Lady Angela Thorpe was suffering agonies of mortification. She had not seen the Viscount alone since his generous bestowal of the diamond bracelet, and several of her perfumed notes had languished unanswered, despite passionate pleas for an immediate rendezvous. On the other hand, an exorbitant bill from the mantua-maker had been met by the Viscount with gratifying promptness, and Lady Angela had not allowed herself to feel seriously worried.

Now, however, she could see the new Vicountess Blackwood for herself, and it was no longer possible to deny the unwelcome accumulation of evidence in front of her own eyes. Viscountess Blackwood was about to become a social hit—the latest and most glittering star on the London horizon. Lady Angela, dancing and laughing and flirting as if she had not a care in the world, watched Sarah and her heart almost burst with rage. She was not a fool, and she did not try to deceive herself. Sarah's slim figure attracted all eyes, and her quiet voice commanded attention without effort. Her laughter lit up the ivory pallor of her complexion with a becoming sparkle, drawing those around her into the circle of her merriment. Beneath it all, her enormous eyes hinted a a passion lurking below the cool modesty of her demeanour. Society, Lady Angela quickly saw, was entranced by this fresh and delicate beauty.

Worst of all, although the Viscount and his wife had no even danced with one another after the opening set, Lady Angela's jealous eyes could not miss the covert attention each gave to the other. The Viscountess might laugh and dance with a dozen different gentlemen, but her gaze constantly returned to the Viscount. He, in turn, was playing the perfect host, but Lady Angela bitterly observed the smiles which passed between the couple every time their eyes chanced to meet. Her pleasure in the diamond bracelet flashing on her arm turned into ashes. The new pink ballgown offered her no comfort. The natural caution which had helped to conceal her true nature from the Viscount through almost two years of intrigue and clandestine meetings, entirely deserted her. She was aware of nothing save a desire to lash out and to wound the women who had usurped her place at the Viscount's side.

It was unfortunate for Lady Angela that the Viscount chose to claim her as his partner just at the moment when rage finally exploded through the barriers of her natural cunning. She managed one false trill of laughter as he offered her his arm and, looking at him coquettishly through drooping eyelashes, she complimented him upon Lady Blackwood's charming appearance.

"Thank you," said the Viscount curtly. He was obscurely offended by Lady Angela's remark, and he found himself repelled by the cloying strength of her perfume as she pressed her body improperly close to his own. Dispassionately, he viewed the elaborate hairstyle, the over-abundance of jewels and the sumptuous lace of her gown. In a moment of shock he saw her as she would be in a few years' time: over-painted, blowsy, clinging desperately to a vanished youth and beauty which was all she had ever had to offer.

Her laughter, a little shrill on this occasion, broke into his thoughts.

"It is a pity you did not think to provide your wife with some proper jewels, Everett. Even if she had nothing of her own, you could surely have spared her *something* from the family treasure chest." Unthinkingly, her eyes slid down to the bracelet sparkling on her wrist.

The Viscount looked at her coldly.

"Lady Blackwood does not require jewels to burnish up her appearance, Angela. She possesses qualities that obviate the need for artificial adornment." His voice was silky, but Lady Angela did not miss the hint of steel. "I think, my dear Angela, that you forget yourself in addressing such comments to me. Lady Blackwood is my *wife*."

The subtle emphasis on this final word brought a flush of angry colour to Lady Angela's cheeks.

"Oh la, my lord! I'm sure I meant nothing of any consequence."

"I think, my dear, that you rarely do. Mean anything of consequence, that is."

Lady Angela saw, too late, that she had been foolish. Rage, however potent, must be made subservient to the realities of her financial position. Sir Henry Thorpe had failed to provide for his widow in anything like the manner she had hoped for when she agreed to marry him.

"Everett," she whispered huskily. "Can you not see that I am pining for your attention? It is so long since you have been alone with me."

Gently, the Viscount placed her at arm's length.

"Regrettably, Angela, we are still not alone. Therefore I feel we should abide by the conventions of the dance." He smiled at her in a friendly fashion. "Come, Angela, we have known one another for a long time. Let us remain on good terms, without reproaches for one another."

He was not aware that with these words he mentally dismissed Lady Angela from her position as his mistress. He was only conscious of unusual irritation and a feeling that he would prefer to be dancing with Sarah rather than arguing with Lady Angela. When he spoke the casual words, his conscious wish was merely to ensure that no obvious impropriety should ruffle the surface of his mother's party.

But Lady Angela's whole life had been made up of interpreting hints and responding to moods, and she was immediately alert to the significance of his mildly chiding tones. She had never previously been addressed by the Viscount as if she were a fractious child. In desperation, she made the fatal error of trying to render him jealous.

"Lord Ross has asked me to accompany him to Italy," she said archly. "I have been thinking that perhaps I would be wise to avoid the chill of an English spring."

The Viscount was shaken by the acute sensation of relief which swept through him. Quite kindly, he looked down into Lady Angela's round blue eyes. He needed scarcely a moment to ponder his reply to the unspoken question.

"I think you should accept his offer, my dear. Now that Bonaparte is safely locked up, there is no reason why the Continent should be deprived of a glimpse of your charms." His voice was gentle. "You must allow me the honour of providing you with some clothes. You will need a new wardrobe for such a prolonged journey."

Lady Angela was torn between fury at this indifferent dismissal of a two-year old liaison, and gratification that some profit still remained in the relationship. Her eyes travelled involuntarily to Sarah, who waltzed round the ballroom in the arms of old Sir William Haversham, a man who acknowledged Lady Angela with the curtest of bows. One person, she reflected bitterly, was the source of her present misery. Had it not been for Sarah, she might even now be receiving the good wishes of the Viscount's friends. Sir William would be dancing with *her*, and not with the pale skinny girl the Viscount had unaccountably married. A career as a *demi-mondaine* loomed uninvitingly before her. The loss of her position as the future Viscountess Blackwood hurt even more than the loss of the Viscount himself, although—as she already knew—Lord Ross was too old to replace the Viscount as a satisfactory lover.

With an effort she tore her attention away from Sarah's twirling figure. Lady Angela had a long memory for injuries, and some opportunity for revenge against the Viscountess would eventually occur. In the meantime, it was necessary to extract the maximum profit possible from the deep purse of the Viscount. She allowed a sad smile to tremble on her lips. Her voice almost broke on a convincing half-sob, hastily suppressed.

"Ah, Everett! The sunshine of Italy will seem cold without you beside me."

"You must remember to take a fur wrap, my dear."

Her blue eyes opened very wide. "But I do not have one, my lord."

"I seem to remember that there is a charming cape of white ermine which we both saw in Madame Boucher's establishment." He smiled at her cynically. "Please permit me to offer it as a substitute for the warmth of my presence."

The dance ended and she swept him a low curtsey.

"My lord, your generosity overwhelms me. What should I say?"

"If I were you," said the Viscount impatiently, "I should just say thank you."

Sarah's happiness at the success of the ball was marred by only two small flaws. First, the impossibility of remembering all her partners' names, and secondly, the fact that the Viscount showed no desire to dance with her a second time. Moving laughingly from one flirtatious partner to the next, however, it was relatively easy to put these minor aggravations from the forefront of her mind. Even when she saw him cross the floor to take Lady Angela into his arms for the waltz, she managed to laugh and smile as cheerfully as ever. Her partner, spellbound by the dreamy mystery of her grey eyes, scarcely noticed that her replies to his questions rarely extended beyond a monosyllabic "yes" or "no". He rejoined his companions, perfectly content to add to the swelling ranks of Lady Blackwood's lovelorn admirers.

The evening was drawing almost to a close when she turned to greet her partner for the minuet. As her eyes searched out the Viscount's tall figure, she noted absently that her new partner was a slender man, pale complexioned and rather older than many of the young sprigs who had claimed her attention during the course of the night. He bowed slowly over her outstretched hands, and allowed his gaze to linger in open admiration upon Sarah's flushed cheeks and dreamy eyes. The Viscount was seen to escort Lady Babbington in the direction of the refreshments, and Sarah was at liberty to bring her attention back to her partner. He bowed again politely as he escorted her into the set.

"I am delighted you have remembered our engagement, my lady. You were surrounded by such a court of admirers when we were introduced that I feared I would have to leave your delightful party without experiencing the pleasure of dancing with you."

Sarah smiled. "I have certainly remembered our agreement to dance, sir. But I have to confess that I do not recall hearing your name. You will have to forgive me, if you please."

"It is not at all surprising that you do not remember. You have been surrounded all evening by a sea of admiring faces. Mine was merely one among many. I am Baron Tynsdale of Greenside."

Some of the colour left Sarah's cheeks, but she smiled prettily, and her voice was quite steady when she spoke.

"We must take our positions, my lord. The musicians are almost ready to begin."

"It will be my pleasure." He offered his arm and if he felt the tremble of her fingers as they rested on his sleeve, he made no mention of the fact. He smiled at her politely.

"Now, you must tell me how it came about that my friend Blackwood managed to steal a march on us all by marrying the prettiest girl in England before she ever appeared in London. I assume you have not been living in London?"

Some version of this conversation had already taken place with virtually every one of her previous partners. Now, however, Sarah found that the story of her marriage did not flow readily from her lips.

"My guardian was a parson, my lord. The Viscount met me while we were both engaged upon charitable work in the parish."

"You amaze me, Lady Blackwood. I would not have thought that my friend Blackwood—admirable fellow though he is—would have concerned himself overmuch with personal works of charity."

Sarah was grateful to grasp at the moment's respite offered when they were separated by the movements of the dance. When they came together again, she answered the Baron briefly.

"The Viscount has not published news of his charitable works to his general acquaintance, my lord. He has not felt the need to do so." Anxious to give substance to her tale, she spoke recklessly. "Why, even now, my husband is caring for a poor old woman whom he rescued from death by neglect in St. Katharine's Workhouse. The Viscount's kindness has been vastly underrated, I think."

"Indeed it has," murmured Baron Tynsdale. "And am I to take it that you share his interest in the . . . er . . . occupants of workhouses?"

"I have already mentioned to you, my lord, that my guardian was a minister of the Church. We lived in London and naturally my upbringing has given me a wider experience of the poverty and misery prevalent in our streets than comes to most young girls." She lifted her head and said formally, "Could we not talk of some other matter? I do not think workhouses and balls mix very comfortably together."

Immediately the Baron was all contrition. He bowed low in a gesture of apology.

"You are absolutely right, my lady. Here I am dancing with the most lovely young woman in the room. How could I choose to discuss anything other than the delightful shade of turquoise you have selected for your gown? The effect upon the colour of your eyes is quite ravishing, my dear Lady Blackwood. You are blessed with most unusual colouring. Is it a frequent combination in your family, this golden-brown hair and dark grey eyes?"

"I am considered to take after my father's side of the family, my lord."

"Ah yes. The Smith family, was it not? I believe I have not had the great pleasure of meeting your father."

"Smith was the name of my guardian. My father and mother are dead."

"And in the twinkling of an eye—or so it appears to those of us who have not been privileged to watch the progress of your romance with the Viscount—you are transformed from an orphan into the Viscountess Blackwood. A charming tale, is it not? Almost like a fairy-tale, in fact."

White-cheeked, Sarah stared at her partner defiantly.

"It is indeed a fairy-tale, my lord. And like most tales of its kind, I intend that this one shall have a happy ending."

"Such fierceness, Lady Blackwood! Why, all of London wishes you success in your new rôle. It is not every one who would be prepared to take on the task of taming my friend Blackwood." His eyes wandered in the direction of Lady Angela. He turned back to Sarah and smiled. "But I am sure you will prove equal to the challenge."

Sarah's chin was raised a fraction higher. "Your solicitude is unnecessary, my lord. Where I am concerned, the Viscount is already tamed."

"I understand completely. And his dance with Lady Angela was in the nature of a farewell. Ah! The music is ended, alas. Where may I escort you now, my lady?"

"Why, to my husband, of course. The last dance has naturally been reserved for him."

He bowed deeply. "Our conversation has been a pleasure, my lady, and opened my eyes to a whole new aspect of my friend's character."

Sarah met his gaze squarely. "I am relieved if I have been

able to disabuse your mind of any misunderstandings, my lord." She almost ran across the few feet of floor which remained to separate her from the Viscount.

"Everett!" she said quickly. "Lord Tynsdale has brought me to your side so that I may claim you as my partner for the last dance." She looked at him with silent appeal. "You remember that we agreed to save the last waltz for each other."

"But of course I remember," said the Viscount smoothly. "How could I forget such an important commitment?" He turned to greet the Baron. "And how convenient that you should be here, Tynsdale. Lady Angela has just informed me that she wilts for lack of a glass of champagne. May I entrust you with the task of procuring a glass for her?"

Baron Tynsdale inclined his head politely.

"It is always my pleasure to be of service to Lady Thorpe. And to you, of course, my dear Blackwood."

He turned to Sarah and raised her hands to his lips.

"Lady Blackwood, it has indeed been a delightful encounter. I trust that it will not be long before we are again enjoying one another's company. I must not lose track of you now that my friend the Viscount has so kindly brought you to my attention." He smiled gently into the veiled hostility of the Viscount's gaze and, offering his arm to Lady Angela, escorted her with swift efficiency in the direction of the dining-room buffet. Sarah watched his departure with mesmerized intensity, and shivered as his dark blue coat passed out of view.

The Viscount walked slowly back in the direction of the dance floor. "You might be good enought, Sarah, to enlighten me as to what that was all about."

"I don't know, my lord. He frightened me. That is why I came to your side. In almost every sentence he called you his friend, yet I think he is not your friend at all."

The Viscount shrugged. "We are acquaintances only. Politically, I cannot agree with his views. But he is a man of considerable consequence among the *ton*. He is not a wise man to offend."

"I did not wish to spend any more time with him. I hope I did not interrupt some important conversation?"

"Lady Thorpe and I have nothing more to say to one another." He looked down at the top of her head, which was all he could see since her eyes were determinedly lowered. He spoke impatiently. "I am flattered that you should find my waistcoat buttons so entirely fascinating: I had not realized their design was so unique."

He waited a moment for her to speak, but when she remained silent, he said curtly, "You called me Everett a few minutes ago."

"I was agitated, my lord. I will not repeat the mistake."

"On the contrary, I insist that you do so whenever we are alone together. I do not enjoy a great deal of pomp in my bedroom."

Sarah's feet lost themselves in one of the turns of the waltz, and only the firm hands of the Viscount prevented her from tripping.

"And I was just thinking how grateful I should be to the dancing master for his excellent tuition!" There was no mistaking the hint of laughter in his voice.

She regained her composure rapidly. "There is a slight unevenness in the floor just at that point. I shall make mention of it to the Dowager Viscountess tomorrow morning."

"An excellent idea," agreed the Viscount gravely. They took two or three silent turns around the floor.

"Where are we going?" exclaimed Sarah suddenly.

"I thought you looked a trifle warm," said the Viscount suavely. "A few moments in the conservatory will serve to refresh you before we attempt the journey home."

"But I am already at home!"

"No, my dear. You are a guest in my mother's house. Tonight you will be returning with me to my house. *That* is your home."

She was silent, and turned away to fan herself.

"How thoughtful of my mother to have provided us with such very large palm trees," said the Viscount conversationally.

Sarah turned round. "Why is that, my lord?"

"It will offer us such an excellent screen when I kiss you," said the Viscount.

Sarah started to move away, but found herself held firmly by two powerful hands.

"Sarah Smith, you are certainly a witch who has been sent to torment me. But I am going to make sure that you do not come out of this encounter totally unscathed."

She did not try to make any sensible response to this somewhat enigmatic statement, for the Viscount's lips now hovered tantalizingly close to her own, and Sarah found it quite essential to reserve all her strength for the difficult task of breathing. She closed her eyes and felt his mouth dash a gentle touch across the lids, then all her conscious thoughts were obliterated as he claimed her in a kiss of passionate intensity.

She could not tell how many minutes passed by before she rested her head against the starched frills of his shirtfront, deriving a strange comfort from feeling the scratchy fabric against her cheek. She searched her mind for some casual remark that might disguise the intensity of her response to his love-making, but her thoughts remained in an unhelpful whirl of excitement.

It was the Viscount who broke the silence. He gave an oddly hesitant laugh, although the hand which caressed her hair seemed steady enough. He looked down into Sarah's eyes.

"Well, witch, I am not sure whether to consider that a successful experiment. Perhaps we should repeat the test."

"No!" She was panic-stricken at the thought of any further onslaught upon her weakened defences. She needed time to harden her heart against the nonchalant expertise of his kisses. "My lord, we shall certainly be seen."

He smiled ruefully. "I do not believe that it is considered a crime to kiss one's own wife. Not, perhaps, a fashionable occupation. But to the best of my knowledge it has not yet been declared illegal."

She managed a small laugh. "My lord, you are absurd. Besides, you know that I am not really your wife."

Even in the semi-darkness of the conservatory, she could see the supercilious questioning of his expression.

"And what might that remark mean, may I ask?"

"My lord, we cannot discuss it here. You know very well what I mean. It was an accident—the merest whim of fate that threw us together."

"That is certainly true," agreed the Viscount readily. "I have been congratulating myself upon the benevolence of my guiding stars for the last several days. After all, I might have decided to marry Lizzie!"

She wished that she could believe him and place her trust in the half-serious tones which underlay his mocking voice. She closed her eyes for an instant and felt again the icy black waters of the Thames swirling above her head, heard the soft, cultured voice of the man who ordered her captors to drown her. If only her eyes had not been covered during those long days of captivity! If only the Viscount would give her some rational explanation of his extraordinary action in marrying her!

She opened her eyes and found the Viscount's gaze fixed rigidly upon her whitened cheeks. There was no longer any laughter in his eyes.

"Come," he said brusquely, "it is past the time when you should be home. We shall make our farewells to my mother. I have been negligent in forgetting that you are still weakened from the after-effects of your fever."

She did not protest, but allowed him to lead her back into the ballroom. The crowd had thinned at last, and the Dowager was chatting with evident contentment to Lady Amelia and her son-in-law.

The Viscount raised both the Dowager's hands to his lips.

"Mama, your party was magnificent as of course I knew it would be. Sarah and I have come to offer you our thanks and to bid you good-night. We must return to my house so that Sarah may get some rest. I have allowed her to become over-tired."

The Dowager Viscountess made no comment upon this precipitate departure of her house-guest, but simply turned very bright eyes in Sarah's direction.

"Well, my dear," she said. "How does it feel to be the new Success of the Season?"

Sarah's cheeks coloured faintly, but she said cheerfully. "You should know, ma'am, for it is *your* party which is going to become the talk of the town."

The Dowager stood up and pressed her cheek against Sarah's. "I shall miss you," she said. "Make sure that Everett takes proper care of you."

The Viscount interrupted, speaking with exaggerated calm. "We are driving five minutes across town, Mama. I am not planning to set out with Sarah for a journey to the South Seas. And naturally I am planning to take care of Sarah. Dr. Thompson has already made arrangements to visit us tomorrow." He shook Sir George firmly by the hand, and dropped a brotherly peck absent-mindedly upon Lady Amelia's cheek. His glance softened again as he turned back to Sarah.

"Are you ready?" he asked briefly.

She nodded silently, embraced the Dowager again and curtseyed politely to her brother and sister-in-law. The Viscount placed a firm arm beneath her elbow, and ushered her from the room. Lady Amelia watched their departure with some amusement.

"I never thought to see Everett hopelessly in love." She looked anxiously at her mother. "Do you think Sarah cares for him at all? She is charming, but it is impossible to read behind that screen of polite reserve."

The Dowager seemed at her most vague. "Such a dear girl, and so helpful with the arrangements for this ball. And so fortunate that Lady Angela decided to wear pink, don't you agree? There cannot possibly be a colour which is less becoming now that she is getting a little fat."

She beamed up at Sir George, whose eyes twinkled shrewdly. "I do believe that the old Duke of Shropshire is still here, Sir George. I must request your arm to escort me to him. I have not seen him stay this late at a party since he gave up making a fool of himself over Julia Throgmorton."

"It will be my pleasure," said Sir George. "But unless you wish to offend all your acquaintances, I should endeavour, ma'am, to look a little less like the cat who has just swallowed a large dish of the very best cream."

The Dowager seemed hurt. "What can you mean, Sir George? It is surely not my fault that Lady Angela becomes a little stout?"

"It seems hardly possible," agreed Sir George. "But I would not put most other meddling outside the scope of your achievements."

"I'm sure I don't understand you." The Dowager's face was a study in innocence. "It is well known that I haven't a brain inside my head. I am entirely dependent upon the men in my family."

"That is certainly well-known, ma'am. And for almost a week after we first met, you even convinced me."

The Dowager Viscountess smiled mischievously.

"Ah, Sir George! I have always said that your talents are wasted down in Kent!"

TWELVE

The maid brushed Sarah's hair with swift, efficient strokes, admiring the luxuriant richness of the golden-brown curls. Sarah stirred restlessly in her chair, wishing she could break the respectful silence that reigned in the great bedchamber. Aggie Meadows was still at the Dowager's town house, and tonight she missed her old housekeeper's familiar chatter.

It was late, well past two in the morning, and she ought to feel tired, but sleep had rarely seemed further away. Impressions of the ball whirled through her mind in a brilliant kaleidoscope of images, with the obscurely threatening figure of Baron Tynsdale running as a dark thread through them all. Silently she debated within herself. Should she seek out the Viscount tomorrow and tell him the truth? After all, did she have anything to lose by such a step? If the Viscount was part of a conspiracy against her—and how absurd that seemed—would he not already know of her connection to the Baron?

The maid tied the ribbons of Sarah's nightgown, drawing a white silk dressing-gown over her shoulders. Sarah sighed wistfully as the maid closed the row of tiny buttons. The memory of the Viscount's kisses kept coming back to torment her and, for at least the hundredth time, she wished that her previous experience of men had been a little wider. Her parents had been dead for more than six years and life with her dear, unworldly uncle had not exposed her to many of the lusts and joys of ordinary men.

A wry smile hovered around Sarah's lips. Brought up by two such paragons of virtue as her uncle and sister, she was not very well equipped for resisting the appeal of the Viscount's expert love-making. It had not previously occurred to her—and certainly would never have occurred to Uncle Charles—that it was quite possible to feel an overwhelming urge to be kissed by a man whose character undoubtedly left a great deal to be desired.

She sighed again as she recalled the sudden tenderness in the Viscount's expression when they had been alone together in the conservatory. She remembered the comfort of his arms as she had rested against him in the carriage tonight. It was simply not possible to believe that he was the man who had callously ordered her death by drowning, whatever his strange motives in entering this marriage.

The maid gave a final twitch to the folds of Sarah's gown, blowing out the candles set on the dressing-table.

"Do you wish me to turn out the lamps, my lady?"

With an effort, Sarah dragged her thoughts back to the matters at hand. She supposed she ought to go to bed.

"No," she said. "I am going to read for a while."

"Very well, my lady."

The maid said nothing to indicate her true feelings about people who sat up reading books at three in the morning. After a lifetime in service, the ways of the Quality still remained an absolute mystery to her practical mind.

"Good-night, my lady."

Sarah replied absent-mindedly, and wandered over to the fire. It was ridiculous to be out of bed at this hour of the night and, despite the robustness of her general constitution, probably unhealthy as well. When she heard a light tap at the door, she would not admit to herself that this was the sound for which she had been waiting.

"Who is it?" she called out, as if there were actually some doubt in her mind.

The Viscount came into the room without bothering to answer her question. He was dressed in a long crimson robe which swept the floor as he walked slowly towards her. The high velvet collar did not quite conceal the fact that he wore no cravat. Sarah stared at the naked expanse of his throat in silence; she had never before seen a man without his cravat. He did not stop until he was so close to her that the swansdown trimming of her dressing-gown brushed against the brocade of his robe.

"Why are you here?" Sarah's heart was beating so thunderously in her ears that the question sounded scarcely louder than a whisper.

"I should have thought that was obvious," said the Viscount. He seemed amused.

Sarah turned hastily towards the flickering flames of the fire. "I couldn't sleep," she said. Her voice was strangely breathless. "One's first ball is always an excitement, you know."

"It is so long ago since I was at my first dance that I had forgotten." His voice was indulgent. "Did you enjoy it?"

"Yes, thank you." She turned round to smile at him shyly. "I hope you were pleased with . . . everything?"

"Not with everything. I found that I was obliged to spend too much time being polite to respectable dowagers, It drastically reduced the time I had available for—er—refreshing myself in the conservatory."

"My lord . . ."

"My name is Everett. Why are you trembling? Are you cold?"

"Yes. I don't know. I must be cold if I am shivering."

Without saying another word, he picked her up in his arms and carried her across to the bed. He placed her gently among the soft pillows, tucking the covers tightly around her.

"Sarah," he said quietly, and took both her hands between his own. "If you wish me to leave, I will do so."

She said nothing, and he leant across the bed, capturing her beneath the weight of his body. His eyes burned with sudden passion, and Sarah was immediately aware of the answering fire that blazed through her body. She tried to steady her ragged breathing so that she might say something—anything—to break the spell. He put out a finger and stroked the curve of her cheek and the long smooth line of her throat.

"I think it is already too late for you to send me away," he said, and his smile enveloped her in its warmth. "We have been married for almost a month, Sarah. Are you ready to become my wife?"

His lips met hers in a fierce question, and she responded to his kiss without reserve. Her hands tangled in his hair as she held him to her, and she sighed with pleasure as his mouth caressed her throat, her eyes and the soft skin of her shoulders.

"You are beautiful," he whispered, and she felt lost in the surging sea of sensations aroused by his lingering touch. She knew now that she had yearned secretly for the feel of his arms around her, and that her body had ached for a fulfilment that she scarcely understood. Through a mist of passion she heard his voice, low and urgent.

"Say that you want me, Sarah. Say that you want me as your husband."

"I love you, Everett." The words were not what she had intended to say, but apparently they answered his question, for with a small cry of triumph, he gathered her into his arms. Her conscious thoughts, her hesitations, her will to resist were all swept away, drowned in the rushing wave of mingled pain and ecstasy.

The first light of dawn was already breaking through a chink in the heavy satin curtains when she woke and stirred in his arms. The Viscount got out of bed immediately and searched on the floor for her robe, wrapping her up swiftly in the soft folds of swansdown.

"I keep forgetting that you have been ill," he said. "Although nobody looking at you now could believe what a scarecrow I married!" He touched her affectionately on the cheek. "Are you too tired to talk to me, just for a little while? I think the time has come to make certain matters plain between the two of us."

She shook her head. She was afraid to speak in case her voice betrayed her absurd longing to throw herself into his arms yet again. She looked down at the strong fingers covering her own, and then looked hastily away again. Her previous knowledge of love-making might have been limited to a few brief lectures from Cassie, but from these she had learned that gentlemen had animal passions not shared by ladies. She had also been informed that true gentlemen did not expect their wives to respond enthusiastically to the more distressing aspects of married life. Sarah was afraid that she had already betrayed a serious lack of maidenly modesty. She hoped, by the icy calm of her manner, to convey to the Viscount that last night's passionate embraces would never be repeated. She hoped fervently that the Viscount would be willing to gloss over the events of the past few hours without further discussion. It would be painfully humiliating if he felt constrained to rebuke her. She was deeply relieved when the Viscount started to speak, and she realized that his thoughts were centred on quite other matters than the regrettably passionate events of the past night.

"While you were staying with my mother, Sarah, I made several enquiries in your old neighbourhood," he said at last. "I apologize for prying into your past history, but I needed to know something about the woman I had married, and you were not very willing to help! I quickly learned that your guardian had been a dedicated minister, admired by the poor people who made up his congregation. The churchwarden at St. Stephen's is a garrulous old man, Sarah, and he was proud of the fine work performed by the Reverend Charles Smith. He told us all about the Reverend's help to the poor, and about the two young ladies who had started a school for some of the children. We also learned that the Reverend Smith came to London from a parish in Hampshire." He touched her pale cheek gently. "I'm sure you know already, my dear, that the vicar in Hampshire six years ago was a man named Charles Beaufort. He became Charles Smith only when he arrived in London."

He raised her hands to his lips and dropped a gentle kiss into the palm. Sarah, reflecting on this comforting evidence that he did not altogether despise her, almost lost the thread of the conversation. With considerable effort she brought her mind away from the significance of her husband's kisses, and back to the meaning of his words.

"Sarah," he urged her. "There can be no reason for silence between us now. There is no reason for you to struggle to conceal some small scandal in your guardian's past. Lord knows, there are few of us who do not have at least one past action we would rather forget. Can you not trust me with the truth?"

She hesitated only briefly. For days she had wondered whether to confide in him, and now he was actually pleading for her trust. The urge to tell him some of the truth was overwhelming. She took a deep breath and spoke quickly before her resolve could desert her. Her parents had been dead for six years. How could the truth hurt them not?

"My guardian was guilty of no wrong-doing, my lord. He merely wanted to protect my sister and myself from discovery My father was a minister, the brother of Charles Beaufort, so that my name is, in fact, Sarah Beaufort. My mother's story is a familiar one. She fell in love with my father and married him against all the wishes of her family. My grandfather was a proud and vengeful man, who laid great store by wealth and worldly position. He was furious at this act of defiance from his only daughter, especially since she had always seemed a docile young girl. She was cut off without even the proverbial shilling, and I understand her name was expunged from all the family records. Luckily, my father was highly thought of by his bishop and a new position was found for him, well away from my mother's former home. We lived very happily in a parish close to my uncle, until my parents died of consumption within a few months of

each other. When news of their death was printed in the
"Morning Post" a lawyer came to see my Uncle Charles. He
was an envoy from my grandfather, and he wanted to take
Cassie and me back with him to be brought up on the family
estates. But Uncle Charles had been appointed our guardian
by my father, and he rejected the idea of returning us to my
grandfather most strongly. He had heard too many tales of
unhappiness from my mother."

"Was that altogether wise, nevertheless?" asked the Viscount. "I imagine that your mother's family would have
been able to provide you with many material advantages
that your uncle could not."

"Uncle Charles never considered sending us back to the
family which had rejected our mother so callously only
fifteen years previously. He believed his love for us quite
outweighed any material advantages my grandfather might
have provided. And my father had left sufficient funds to see
that we were sent to a good school."

"I stand rebuked." The Viscount smiled. "There is no
need to look at me quite so fiercely!"

"When Uncle Charles took us to London, he changed his
name and concealed the fact that we were blood relations.
He wished to make pursuit a little more difficult, if my
grandfather was really determined to find us. My uncle
loved us deeply, but he was dedicated to his work and he
didn't want to spend years of his life making formal claims
for guardianship. He knew how much power my mother's
family could wield. As the Reverend Charles Smith, he
hoped to disappear into the London crowds. As the
Reverend Charles Beaufort, accompanied by two nieces, he
would quickly have been traced by my grandfather. It
became second nature for Cassie and me to conceal our
origins and our family name."

The Viscount still held her hand, stroking it absently with
his thumb. "Am I to be told the name of the family to which
your mother belonged? Or is that still to be considered a

state secret?"

Sarah tugged at the soft trimming of her gown. At last she raised her eyes to the Viscount's face.

"My grandfather was Baron Tynsdale of Greenside. I imagine that the present baron must be my mother's younger brother. His age would be about correct."

The Viscount sprang to his feet, looking at Sarah in silent astonishment.

"So *that* is what was bothering you last night!" he said slowly as he sank into a chair by the fireside. "Forgive my amazement. I had not realized how accurately you spoke when you described your mother's family as powerful. Old Baron Tynsdale was an important member of the Prince Regent's inner circle of advisers."

Sarah shrugged. "I hope his advice to the Prince was more successful than the management of his family's affairs. My mother spoke little of her childhood, but I believe it was extremely unhappy—chiefly because of Baron Tynsdale's violent and erratic temper."

"I did not know him personally," said the Viscount. "He was an elderly man even before I came down from university."

His expression softened as he looked into Sarah's enormous grey eyes, shadowed by fatigue and some other indefinable emotion. "The present Baron Tynsdale is not your uncle, Sarah. I am sorry to have to tell you that your mother's brother died five or six years ago in a hunting accident. It was much commented upon at the time, since your grandfather was an old man and the accident left him without a direct heir. The present baron is quite a distant cousin, I believe. I regret that I must be the one to give you such sad news about your family."

"I never met my mother's brother, my lord, or my grandfather, so how could I feel personal sorrow to learn of their death? In some ways, I actually feel relieved. My mother nourished tender memories of her younger brother, although he was too young to defy my grandfather by seeking us out. When I was introduced to Baron Tynsdale at the ball, I was aware only of a sudden spark of mutual antipathy. I am glad to know that the Baron is only a distant relative and not my uncle."

The Viscount walked slowly away from the fireplace and came to stand once again by the side of the bed. His face was hidden by the shadow of the canopy when he started to speak.

"There is one more question that I have to ask you, Sarah. Why did you not turn to your mother's family when your sister died and your situation became so desperate? Surely it would have been better to humble your pride than to throw yourself into the river? What can your mother have told you, that led you—of all people—to believe that the Tynsdales were such monsters that death was preferable to their protection?"

With a sudden lithe movement, Sarah sprang out of the bed and stood facing the Viscount. Her voice shook with emotion, but her manner was calm.

"No! Enough! Now it is *your* turn, my lord. You have probed into the story of my life, you have questioned me and harassed me so that *your* curiosity might be satisfied. Now it is my turn to be curious, and my justification is greater, I believe. Why were you combing the slums for a bride, my lord? Why did you choose to marry *me?*"

The Viscount turned away, so that Sarah could no longer see his face. "My reasons seemed adequate at the time," he said finally. He turned towards the fire, and a dying ember lit up the wry smile that touched his mouth. "I cannot say that I regret my actions, because if I had behaved rationally I would never have married you. Can you not accept that it was a stroke of miraculous good fortune for us both? You were rescued from death and I . . ." He paused for a moment, then laughed quietly. "I do believe that I was saved from a fate worse than death, although I did not realize it at the time."

"Riddles!" said Sarah scornfully. "You are very entertaining, my lord, but not very informative. It does not please me to find myself married to a man who insists that I should be frank, but who himself conceals the truth." She tossed her head angrily, and her long hair shimmered around her shoulders in a golden-brown halo of colour. "You have yourself shown me the way out of my dilemma. I am not friendless; I am not without a family to support me. You speak of the power of the Tynsdales. Unless you tell me why you married me my lord, I shall seek the protection of my mother's family!"

"Your threat would be more convincing, madam, if you did not deliver it a scant hour after you have welcomed me into your bed. Last night I did not find you over-anxious to seek protection from my embraces!" He seized her roughly by the arms, forcing up her chin so that he could stare down into her tear-filled eyes.

"What's the use of pretending?" he said harshly. "You have asked for the truth and so you shall have it. I wished to become a widower, and I selected you as my bride because I believed that you would die during the night following our wedding ceremony. I hope, madam, that you are satisfied with the explanation you demanded."

Sarah's cheeks blanched to a colour as pale as the white of her robe. "But why did you allow me to survive?" she whispered.

"That, madam, is a question I have frequently asked myself. I have not yet arrived at a satisfactory answer."

The door of the bedchamber slammed behind him, and Sarah was left to rejoice in the satisfaction of having extracted from her husband precisely the information which she least wished to hear.

THIRTEEN

Baron Tynsdale of Greenside, unlike Viscount Blackwood, was not given to displays of temper. His servants, however, knew better than to ignore even the most softly-spoken of his orders. They had learned from painful experience that a quiet voice and mild manners could conceal a ruthless will and a cold heart.

On the day after the Blackwoods' ball, word was swiftly passed round the servants' hall warning that the master was in a rare old mood and not to be crossed. The servants scurried about their duties with silent urgency and, despite the fact that the Baron never once raised his voice above a low murmur, each servant dreaded a summons into the master's presence.

There was nobody, from the new scullery-boy up to the butler himself, who did not feel lighter of spirit when the Baron called for a hackney carriage and set off for some unspecified destination, carrying a small portmanteau. There was a general wish, unexpressed for fear of the consequences, that it might be several days before the Baron returned to his house.

The hackney carried its passenger through the fashionable streets of London's West End, still empty at this early hour of the morning, and crossed over into the City, finally coming to a halt outside an old but respectable warehouse on the fringes of Cheapside. The Baron paid his fare in silence and entered the gloomy doorway of the building. The driver, wondering idly what a regular swell was doing visiting a warehouse, was still trotting his horse slowly down the street when a clerk, hunched against the cold, emerged from the shadowed door of the building.

Baron Tynsdale, changed into a shabby black suit, his figure muffled in the folds of a heavy felt cape, walked briskly past the hackney. He did not pause to glance at the driver, for the possibility of recognition did not occur to him.

He attracted no attention as he walked at an even pace through the streets of the City, and only halted when he reached a tumble-down tavern almost on the wharf of St. Katherine's dockyard. Although modestly dressed, with his broad-brimmed hat and old cloak showing considerable signs of wear, in this part of town his clothing marked him as a stranger. Most of the other passers-by on the wharf looked gaunt from chronic under-feeding, and pinched by the bitter chill of the March wind. He hurried inside the tavern, unwilling to call attention to himself despite the pistol he held ready cocked in his hand.

It was some time before his eyes adjusted to the gloom of the tavern's interior. It was difficult, at first, to see through the grey fog of smoke belching out from the fireplace and from the clay pipes of tobacco. Eventually, however, his smarting eyes found the man for whom he searched. Without undue haste he got up from his seat on the bench and strolled over to an old stevedore, whose rounded cheeks spoke of access to a more plentiful food supply than some of his neighbours.

The Baron stood quietly beside him, saying nothing, until awareness of an alien presence finally penetrated the gin-soaked brain of the stevedore. The old man peered drunkenly at the cloaked figure standing close to the table, and a cracked grin spread across his toothless gums.

"Got another job for us, guv'nor? Me and Squiffy would be real 'appy to 'elp you out."

"I wish to speak to you outside." The Baron turned and left the tavern, not bothering to wait and see if his command was obeyed. The stevedore grinned somewhat sheepishly at his drinking companions. It did not look well to jump fast to such a softly-spoken suggestion. Nevertheless, he lurched to his feet and hurried out into the miserable drizzle of the March afternoon.

The Baron offered no word of greeting. "I paid you to . . . dispose . . . of something for me," he said briefly. "You did not do so."

Righteous indignation, mingled with a touch of fear, appeared on the stevedore's face.

"Yes we did!" he exclaimed. "We took the wench right down on to the embankment, just the two of us. Course, we didn't tie her up nor nothin' on account of how you wanted it to look like she done herself in. But we threw her right out into the middle o' the river. And that's the 'onest truth, guv'nor."

"But she was not dead when she went into the river. She cannot have been, for I have seen her since."

"She were as good as dead, guv'nor, and that's the truth. Hardly breathing when we threw her in. Sank to the bottom like a stone. Ain't no way she could 'ave come out alive. Besides, it's too deep there. She'd have to swim to get out of the water, and whoever 'eard of a girl swimming?" He cackled nervously, and risked a glance at the face of his sometime employer.

The Baron's face was muffled between the brim of his hat and the collar of his coat. In the misty light of the dockside it was impossible to guess at his thoughts.

"Which is the nearest infirmary to this dock?" he asked.

The stevedore looked at him pityingly. "Ain't none in this part o' town," he said. "If you're unlucky, somebody might take you into the workhouse. That's a quick way to die, if ever you wants one."

For a moment, it seemed that a flash of interest had flared in the Baron's cold eyes, but it might have been no more than a trick of the light.

"Whereabouts in the river did you . . . dispose . . . of the body?" he asked. "Which would be the closest workhouse?"

"I reckon St. Katherine's would be as close as any," said

the stevedore.

"You were paid to do a job and failed to do it. Take care that no word of our—dealings—should ever leak out. I would see you to Tyburn very quickly, my friend. If you must drink gin, make sure that it does not wet your tongue too much. And thank God that you were never foolish enought to ask my name." He smiled grimly. "I do not have room in my plans for those who fail me."

The stevedore who, from one cause or another, had killed more men than he could comfortably remember, shivered.

"It's cold out here, guv'nor. I'll be getting back to me mates."

The Baron started to walk away. "I gave you two golden sovereigns to dispose of my unwanted property," he said over his shoulder. "I do not think it would cost me one quarter that sum to have you silenced permanently. Remember that fact if ever you should feel the urge to speak out."

The stevedore crept back into the warmth of the dark and dingy tavern. The noisy shrieks and ribald laughter of his companions had never before sounded so welcome.

Mrs. Gresham retied the ribbons on her frilly cap. They were a bit dirty, not having received the benefit of soap and water since the first of the month, but Mrs. Gresham was well-pleased with the general effect. She greeted her visitor, conscious of looking at her very best. Despite his shabby clothes, he was an aristocrat, or she was mistaken. And it wasn't much more than a month since the last lot had come calling.

The gentleman bowed slightly, and as she sank into a properly respectful curtsey, her eyes happened to light on the golden sovereign, miraculously resting on the edge of her little table. She looked up at her visitor with renewed appreciation, but she said nothing about the money.

"I know you must be a busy woman, Mrs. Gresham, so I

won't take up much of your time." His eyes slid over to the beautiful golden coin. "I hope you will accept a little token of my thanks for the help you are going to give me."

"It's a pleasure, sir." She did not bother to ask what help she was supposed to give. Her hand slipped along the surface of the table and closed on the gratifying solidity of the golden coin. "What do you want me to do?"

"I am looking for a young woman," he said abruptly. "Less than twenty, thin, brown hair, grey eyes. She was here about a month ago. I expect she was brought in out of the River Thames."

Mrs. Gresham was suddenly wary. Two sets of men, both asking about the same girl. This, surely, would prove in the end to be worth more than a single sovereign. Her expression became blank, her little eyes veiled in stupidity.

"We have so many young girls, sir. We must have a round dozen of 'em right at the moment. Why was you particular about wanting this girl, sir? I don't know as how I can bring one special girl to mind. We get them fished out of the river here all the time."

"I think, though, that you remember this girl," said the man and his quiet voice sent an odd little ripple tingling down Mrs. Gresham's back. "You see, this girl was removed from here by somebody, a gentleman, I think. I should like to know his name."

Mrs. Gresham sighed. "My memory isn't as good as what it used to be, sir. These young women, they get themselves in the family way, and then it's off into the river before you can say 'Jack Robinson'. Why, only last week there was this young 'un . . ."

"No doubt this will help to refresh your memory. I shall not provide you with anything more, so you may as well give me the information I am seeking."

The matron looked down at the table. A silver crown glinted in a beam of pale sunlight. Her hand reached out to grab it, stuffing it into her pocket alongside the golden sovereign. The two coins made a satisfying jingle as they knocked against one another. It was a pity the second offering was only a crown, but she was too wily a judge of character to hold out for more.

"Funny, but it's all coming back to me now. You must be asking about that poor child, Sarah Smith. Thin little thing, she was, and not even a copper or two tucked into her petticoats. There was two gentlemen what came here more than a month ago. They picked her out of the fever ward and took her away with old Lizzie. Said they wanted to act charitable and provide a good home for a couple of deserving paupers. One of the men was a doctor, keen on poking his nose in what wasn't no business of his. Made me go down the ward personal, givin' all the women drinks of water, although what my paupers had to do with him, I'll never know."

The visitor's impatient voice cut across this flood of reminiscence.

"But their names! Did they give you a name?"

"The tall one, he was a Viscount. Blackwood he said his name was. The doctor was called Thompson, and a toffee-nosed bastard *he* was. Threatening to report my fever ward to the Poor Law Commissioners! And after all I done for them worthless women!"

"Let me set your mind at rest. I am confident that there is little chance Dr. Thompson will wish to reveal his presence here in St. Katherine's Workhouse. You may maintain your usual high standard of care without fear of a visit from the Commissioners. Good evening to you, Mrs. Gresham. I am sure that I need not point out to a woman of your advanced intelligence that there is no need to mention this visit to the beadle . . . or to anyone."

Mrs. Gresham's fingers closed round the reassuring smoothness of the two coins. She'd known Sarah Smith was a troublemaker from the moment the river scavengers had brought her in. Her apple cheeks stretched into an oddly nervous smile.

"Lor' bless you, sir, my memory's that shocking, I've already forgotten you called."

To her delight, a silver florin gleamed suddenly on the dusty surface of the table. "A tribute to your remarkable memory, Mrs. Gresham. I am sure you will put it to excellent use."

The coin dropped into the matron's capacious pocket. She shook her skirts gently and listened to the gratifying rattle of metal upon metal. Four paupers had died today, as well. With their burial allowances, this was going to turn out a profitable week. She hardly noticed the soft opening of the door, and when she glanced up again, her visitor was gone.

Mrs. Gresham sank into the fireside chair and opened a bottle of stout. She spread the three shining coins out on her abundant lap, admiring the warm glow of the gold and the bright shine of the silver. She hoped her visitor wouldn't come back. Even for the sake of twenty-seven shillings, she was not sure that she wanted another encounter with those chilling grey eyes.

The morning was well advanced by the time Baron Tynsdale emerged from the warehouse, his appearance returned to its normal state of unobtrusive elegance. Despite the lateness of the hour, he directed a passing hackney to Lady Angela Thorpe's residence. He seemed untroubled by any thought that his visit could prove unwelcome.

Lady Angela did not keep him waiting for many minutes after his visiting card was handed to the butler. Her curiosity far outweighed any scruples she might have felt at the impropriety of receiving a single man in her private apartments. She tripped into her drawing-room, looking like a creation in spun sugar under the carefully filtered sunlight seeping through the filmy curtains.

The Baron kissed the tips of her fingers, and murmured apologies for the inconvenient hour of his call.

"I was desolated, Lady Angela, to hear from Lord Ross

that you will soon be deserting us for the pleasures of Southern Italy. London will miss your presence and I . . . I shall be particularly sorry to see you go."

"I did not know that you derived such pleasure from my company, Lord Tynsdale." Lady Angela's poise might have deserted her in the face of Viscount Blackwood's defection, but Baron Tynsdale was unlikely to cause her heart to miss a single beat.

"Our interests have not previously coincided," said the Baron smoothly. "Are you quite certain that you wish to go to Italy, Lady Angela?"

She laughed bitterly. "Is there any point in pretending that I have a choice?" She tossed her golden curls angrily. "You saw Viscount Blackwood and his wife at the ball."

Baron Tynsdale toyed abstractedly with the black grosgrain ribbon of his quizzing glass. "I feel that you and I, dear Lady Angela, should speak to one another frankly. It is so difficult to make one's meaning clear if one persists in dancing round the edge of a problem. Let us say that I, for reasons of my own, would prefer Viscount Blackwood to reduce the interest he is showing in his wife's affairs. I confess that it did occur to me that you might be interested in having the Viscount once again unattached?"

"Can you doubt it? But Lady Blackwood. What of her?" Lady Angela could not conceal the venom in her question.

"I think you may rely upon me to take care of the Viscountess. You will have to be content to know that in this, my interests are identical to your own."

"All London knows that I wish Lady Blackwood to the devil. But why should you care if the Viscount has found himself the protegée of a pious parson for his bride?"

"I find that people and events are so rarely what they seem on the surface," said the Baron conversationally. "I will answer your question by saying that Lady Blackwood's past is not without its piquant moments—despite the pious parson. I have business with Lady Blackwood which can better be accomplished without an interested husband to supervise the disposition of her affairs."

He smiled a cold smile, that sent an icy trickle of emotion rippling down Lady Angela's back. "Does that answer your question, my lady?"

She suspected that the Baron wished to pursue a clandestine affair with the Viscountess, but she did not really care about his motives. "Yes, yes," she said impatiently. "It is not important why you wish to discredit her. It is enough that you do. You must have some plan, and I suppose I am to help. What must I do?"

"Your rôle is a simple one, my dear, and I have no doubt will prove quite pleasurable. I wish you to summon the Viscount to your side this evening—and make sure that he does not leave until the morning. I am sure such a task is well within your delightful powers."

"That is all?" Lady Angela turned away so that the Baron would not see her expression. Not for the world would she have revealed the flash of panic-stricken doubt that assailed her. Would she still be able to keep the Viscount's attention for an entire night? Angrily, she brushed the thought aside. How could she have allowed her self-confidence to sink so low? She permitted herself a soft laugh. "You have certainly assigned me a . . . pleasurable . . . task, my lord. What is your own part in the affair to be?"

The Baron laughed. "Why, I take the counterpart to your own rôle, my lady. I shall be entertaining the Viscountess Blackwood. I am anticipating an evening almost as pleasurable as your own."

FOURTEEN

Lady Amelia Sutton parted from Sarah with warm smiles and a sisterly embrace. Their shopping expedition had passed off most agreeably confirming Lady Amelia's opinion that Sarah would prove to be an excellent bride for her arrogant brother. She was perceptive enough to realize that Sarah's soft smiles and pleasant conversation masked a lively intelligence and occasionally sparkling wit. If she also noticed that Sarah's manner was somewhat distraite, and that her eyes were circled by large shadows, she was tactful enough not to comment. Instead, she concentrated her conversation upon the fashionable contents of Sarah's new wardrobe, and chattered inconsequentially about the success of the previous night's ball. Lady Amelia was fond of her brother and curious to know more about the elusive woman who had ousted Lady Angela Thorpe from favour, but she was prepared to wait. So she filled the afternoon with an agreeably rambling account of her children's lively behaviour, and the improvements Sir George had recently put in hand upon the Sutton land.

When she finally settled herself back in the comfortable barouche which had carried them across town, Lady Amelia was somewhat astonished to realize just how little information Sarah had actually offered during the course of their long and friendly outing. The Dowager Viscountess Blackwood when informed of this odd reticence, merely laughed with irritating complacency and said, "I told you you'd get nothing out of her." And with this undeniable truth, Lady Amelia was forced to be content.

Sarah had not in fact, been deliberately reticent with her sister-in-law. Her thoughts, for most of the afternoon, had simply been elsewhere. In between exclaiming at Harry Sutton's prowess on the cricket field, and smiling sympathetically at the antics of two-year-old George, she had decided that the time was overdue to be completely honest with her husband.

When Lady Amelia's barouche set her down in Mount Street, therefore, she did not wait to change out of her pelisse, but slipped into the drawing-room and sent for Potter to ask where she might find the Viscount. Restlessly kneading her French kid gloves into a tight ball, she acknowledged that since she had been foolish enough to fall in love with her husband, he might as well be made aware of her feelings. She was ready to risk telling him the truth about the frightening days preceding her admission into St. Katharine's workhouse, if such frankness could bring back the warm glow into his eyes.

In retrospect, her determined silence seemed rather foolish. If the Viscount was guilty of complicity in an attempt to murder her, then he already knew how she came to be floating in the river. If there should be some other explanation for his strange behaviour—and how desperately she hoped that there was —then cloaking her past in mystery could only perpetuate the ambiguous relationship that existed between them.

Potter's lugubrious expression warned her immediately that the Viscount was not at home, and that he disapproved of the Viscount's destination. Lady Angela Thorpe, she thought miserably. She walked briskly across to the drawing-room window and endeavoured to look as if the budding leaves on the rhododendron bush captivated all her attention.

"Did the Viscount leave word as to when he would be back, Potter?" She hoped her voice sounded sufficiently casual, as if it had slipped the Viscount's mind to remind his wife that he would be late for dinner.

"No, my lady. I'm afraid that I couldn't give you an exact

time when his lordship is expected home."

Potter pursed his lips. He knew very well where the master had gone, chasing off in this curricle just after That Woman's groom had come round with a message. Potter had accepted several hot-pressed notes, addressed in a most vulgar shade of violet ink, during the past two or three weeks and he had been gratified to find these same missives tossed unanswered into his lordship's wastepaper basket. It was disconcerting that this latest letter should have sent the Viscount chasing back to That Woman's side, and just when the whole household had thought her influence entirely at an end. Potter sighed. There was no understanding how the Viscount could prefer such a painted piece of soiled goods in comparison with the lovely young Viscountess. Potter's stern expression cracked into an approximation of a smile.

"Will you be taking dinner in the dining-room, my lady? Or would you like me to have the maids bring you something upstairs? We know that you must be tired, my lady. If I may be permitted to mention it, we have all heard what a triumph you enjoyed at the Dowager Viscountess's party last night."

"Thank you, Potter. Has Aggie Meadows been sent back from Portman Square as yet? If she has, I would like her to come up to my room." She smiled a little wanly. "You are right. I am tired, and I would enjoy eating a quiet dinner upstairs."

A footman arrived before Potter could respond to these instructions. "I have a message for your ladyship," he said, handing her a slim piece of white paper on a silver tray.

Sarah broke the wafer sealing the single sheet of paper, and read the brief message. "Where did you get this?" she asked the footman sharply.

The footman, well trained by Potter, sniffed eloquently.

"It was delivered by a young personage to the back door, my lady. I could ascertain, if you wish, precisely who the person was."

Sarah concealed her slight spurt of amusement, which for

a moment almost overcame her worry. The snobbish instincts of the Viscount's servants would never cease to amuse her.

"Don't bother. It's not important." She turned back to look at the butler. "I have to go out again, Potter, but I expect I shall be back shortly."

"My lady," Potter protested uncertainly. "Will you not take the time to step upstairs and refresh yourself? You have been busy all afternoon, and you are only recently up from your sick-bed."

Sarah looked coolly at the butler. "I have said that I must leave immediately. Perhaps you would hand me my scarf and gloves? I believe it is becoming increasingly chilly outside."

Potter and the footman recognized the unmistakable note of authority behind the crisp words. In disapproving silence, the butler handed his mistress her gloves and scarf, waiting patiently while she retied the strings of her bonnet. When she was once again ready to go out, he escorted her with proper solemnity through the front hall.

As he opened the heavy front door, Potter made one last effort. "May I call the carriage, my lady? Or if you do not have time to wait for it to be brought round, I could send one of the footmen to fetch a hackney."

"I am going to walk, Potter."

The butler watched her brisk walk down the marble entrance steps and out on to the street. The Viscountess turned at the iron railings separating the Blackwood residence from the street, and smiled at him sweetly. With an inward sigh, Potter closed the front door. At least it was still daylight and, with any luck, she would be home again before dusk. Sometimes, just at moments like these, Potter wondered if he was becoming too old for the arduous task of controlling the younger generation of Blackwoods. Who ever would have thought that the Viscountess, such a pale and fragile little thing, would have such a stiff determination? Potter sa down on a chair in the hallway and stared gloomily at his polished black shoes. His legs ached. He was tired.

Sarah walked quickly along the pavement, her feet almost breaking into a run, although she tried to control such an unladylike impulse. Why would Aggie wish to meet her at the corner of Mount Street and the old mews that ran back to St. Peter's Lane? What had the old housekeeper discovered that necessitated this immediate and secret meeting? Although Sarah was well used to walking in parts of London far less salubrious than this elegant section of Mount Street, surely Aggie should realize better than anybody else why she felt so nervous about venturing out totally unaccompanied. Even when helping with her uncle's parish work, she and Cassie had never walked out of the house except in each other's company, or escorted by one of the solid burghers who worked on the Church council.

She was breathless from hurrying when she reached the intersection of the mews and Mount Street, and she paused uncertainly in her tracks. The trees of a nearby garden made this corner darker than the rest of the street. In the fading light, it was almost impossible to see who waited in the dim shadows.

"Aggie?" she called softly. "Aggie, are you there?"

"Over here!" The faint, frightened whisper seemed to come from inside the yard of the corner house. Annoyed by this excessive display of caution, Sarah walked over to the iron gates, ready to remonstrate with the housekeeper.

"Aggie" she said tartly. "Come out from there. That's enough of this play-acting. Whatever has come over you?"

Even as she spoke, a dirty hand was placed over her mouth, and another arm grabbed her around the waist. Struggling desperately, she was swept off the ground and stuffed under the concealing folds of a heavy woollen cloak. A coach rattled out of the gathering darkness of the mews, and she was bundled towards it. Her fingers clawed at the hand which covered her mouth, but to no avail. Defiantly, she bit into the filthy flesh with all the strength she had, and his hand jerked away. Quickly she cried out.

"Help me! Aggie! Help!"

She could say no more, for the filthy hand was clamped again over her mouth, almost covering her nose, and she was thrust roughly into the coach, the door slamming shut behind her.

She jumped up immediately and ran across the floor of the swaying carriage, pulling at the handle of the door, but without success. Wearily, she sank down into a corner seat, looking up to see the cold eyes of Baron Tynsdale fixed frigidly upon her.

"My dear Lady Blackwood, I am so pleased that you decided to respond to the invitation in my little note. I had been waiting for you to come home."

"It was all a trick. Aggie didn't send for me," said Sarah dully. "You recognized me at the ball."

"My dear Lady Blackwood, could you doubt it? Your appearance is not easily forgotten, and I had already enjoyed the pleasure of your company for several days. I found your looks much improved, but not fundamentally altered."

Sarah could not conceal the fear in her eyes, nor could she mask the sudden shiver that shook her body. "It was you!" she whispered. "You were the person who arranged for my . . . who tried to have me killed. But why? I was hardly aware of your existence. I did not even know that my grandfather was dead. I would have made no claims on you."

The Baron laughed sardonically. "Shall we simply say that I found your existence . . . unnecessary? I had high hopes that the fever would take care of you as it did of your sister, but that was not to be. Of course, I had no suspicion of your connection with Viscount Blackwood, no knowledge of your impending marriage, or I should not have attempted such a . . . crude . . . method of disposal. Just how did he come to trace you to St. Katharine's, by the way?"

She ignored his question. Perhaps it was better to let him

believe that her relationship to the Viscount was of long standing. "What are you going to do with me now? Am I going back into the river with a weight around my feet to make sure I do not survive?"

"Tut, tut, my dear cousin. That would hardly be a suitable end for such a shining new light upon the social horizon. Besides, there is just the faintest possibility that your body might be found and identified, and that would be inconvenient for me. I am hoping that we shall be able to come to some comfortable arrangement, just the two of us. I am taking you to my house in Streatham. It is conveniently close to town, and yet also on the route for Dover. You will perceive that it is ideal for our purpose."

"I do not know what your purpose is, my lord."

"I thought I made that perfectly plain the last time we were alone together Ah! We are entering the village already. The coachman has made excellent time. He is a good fellow, although a little uncouth in his habits. My house is adjacent to the grounds of Thrale Hall. My mother was an admirer of Dr. Johnson and tried to establish a salon to rival that of Mrs. Thrale. I am the fortunate inheritor of her house, but not, I am thankful to say, of her literary pretensions."

The coach came to a halt and the door was thrown open without delay. The unprepossessing coachman who had seized her in Mount Street, now barred her exit from the coach. An impassive groom sat on the box of the carriage, pointing a blunderbuss directly at Sarah.

The Baron stepped down into the courtyard and offered his hand courteously to Sarah. His manner seemed little altered from the night before when he had led her out on to the dance floor.

"Pray allow me to escort you inside," said the Baron. "I am afraid you will think my hospitality sadly at fault, but I do assure you that we have done everything possible to make the house comfortable for your needs . . . Please take care as we enter the hallway. I think my housekeeper fears that I will turn her off if she does not polish the floors to a murderous state of waxed cleanliness."

Sarah entered the house lost in a bewildering sensation of unreality. Nothing could have been more innocuous than the Baron's words and gestures, yet this was a man who had admitted to attempting murder.

The bemused state of her feelings was not improved by the strange sensation of familiarity that assailed her senses as they entered the pleasant modern hallway. She looked at the white-panelled walls and the window hangings of striped French blue satin, and knew that she had never seen them before. The Baron did not allow her much time for contemplation. His hand under her elbow propelled her gently but inexorably along the corridor.

He finally stopped outside an elegant, gilt-painted doorway. Bowing politely, he indicated that Sarah should precede him into the room. She had hardly crossed the threshold before she whirled round to face him, her cheeks blanched to a deathly shade of white.

"This is the room," she whispered. "This is where you held me before. I think I can recognize even the smell of it. Why have you brought me here again? How can you hope to keep me confined, when I told my butler that I would be returning within a few minutes?"

Baron Tynsdale shrugged eloquently. "I have taken the precaution of arranging for a message to be delivered to Blackwood House on your behalf. I do not think anybody will find your absence surprising."

"What have you written?" Sarah asked bitterly. "What lies have you told about me this time?"

"My dear Lady Blackwood, we waste precious moments. I am confident that you will now see the wisdom of signing the papers which I shall shortly present for your signature. And as soon as you have signed, I shall be happy to arrange for your return to the bosom of the Blackwood family. Indeed, it will be in my interest to see that you are reinstated as quickly as possible. My friend the Viscount is a stiff-necked sort of fellow, and will not take kindly to a wife who has strayed too long from the nest. I have no desire to raise unnecessary difficulties in your path, Lady Blackwood. Once you have signed the papers, I shall be happy to help you concoct a suitable fairytale to explain what you have been doing."

"And if I do not choose to sign any papers?"

The Baron sat down on a narrow chair and contemplated the tips of his fingers. "I cannot believe that you will persist in such foolishness for long. I need a signature, or proof of your death. Since I do not feel that it would be entirely safe to arrange for your death, I must insist upon the signature. Why should you choose to remain locked up here, languishing in solitary confinement, fed upon bread and water, never absolutely certain when I may decide to cut my losses and make away with you? It would not be the action of a reasonable woman, and I am sure that you are a *most* reasonable woman."

"What do you want me to sign? It must be some document connected with our family. Why are these papers so important to you?"

"Our mutual and revered ancestor was given to certain eccentricities over and above his addiction to the Prince Regent's company. He cast off my cousin, your mother, without a penny and steadfastly refused to hear her name mentioned in his presence. Then his only son died, leaving a wife but no children. The late Baron Tynsdale did not approve of having me as his heir. There was nothing he could do about it, of course, since I was the direct descendant in the male line. But his property was not entailed. He could leave it as he wished."

The Baron laughed mirthlessly. "You can probably imagine my reaction when, having taken pains to see that Richard was killed in the hunting field, I discovered that I had come into an empty inheritance. The title, Greenside

Hall and the home farm are mine. The vast Tynsdale estates, which generate the income that kept all the previous barons in luxury, all that, my dear Lady Blackwood, belongs to you."

There was absolute silence in the room for the space of two heartbeats, then a ripple of laughter escaped from Sarah's lips, rapidly mounting to an hysterical peak. Abruptly she controlled herself, turning her back upon the Baron.

"You will forgive me, my lord. There is a certain irony in your revelations. I am the heir to the Tynsdale fortune, and yet a month ago I was left for dead in a pauper's fever ward." She swung round to face him. "You must know I will not sign, my lord. Neither my mother nor I have ever submitted well to threats."

The Baron rose regretfully to his feet. "I trust that you will shortly change your mind, Lady Blackwood. When you have had a couple of hours for some solitary reflection, you will perhaps decide that there is a difference between your mother's decision to defy a father who posed no real threat to her happiness, and your desire to defy a man who has the power of life and death over you."

"You must take me for a simpleton, my lord. Whatever happens, you will kill me. I shall not be safe for more time than it takes the ink to dry upon your precious papers. Once you have my signature, why should you keep me alive? If you set me free, I can merely return to my husband, insist that the papers were signed under duress, and you are once again deprived of an inheritance."

"There is undoubtedly some truth in what you say, although I think it was unwise of you to point out to me just how little I have to lose by—er—disposing of you. But I have a document already prepared which offers you complete security. It is on the table over there. You may examine it at your leisure. You will find that it contains a full confession of my deeds. You must understand that although there are some men to whom the homeland is everything, I am no such a man. I wish to enjoy the pleasures of life rather than its responsibilities. I do not care for landed estates, or for my family heritage. My title is useful as a seal of social approval; it is nothing more to me. I wish simply to have a large enough income to purchase the services and luxuries that I crave. When you sign over the Tynsdale inheritance to me, you will see that this document guarantees I will remain permanently abroad. The quarterly payments from the estate will be made to me only on condition that I have not been in England during the previous quarter. So you see, if you sign these papers, you will lose some money but you will gain your life. The Viscount is not a poor man, my dear. He is well able to supply you with the trinkets you would like to have. Why risk your survival for the sake of an obstinate streak in your character which should long ago have been brought under control? Obstinacy is so unfeminine, my dear."

She did not trust him for a moment, but now it was essential to get rid of him for a while so that she could try and assimilate the treasure-trove of new facts which he had revealed to her. She could not sift truth from lies while he was scrutinizing her so closely. She ran a fluttering hand across her pale brow, grateful for the fact that her appearance suggested a totally false frailty of constitution.

"I can't think any more," she said in a die-away voice. "I feel so faint, so confused. Please leave me alone for a little while."

He looked at her suspiciously, not being the sort of man to succumb at the first sign of feminine weakness. But there seemed no advantage she could gain by being left to a period of solitary confinement, so he shrugged and spoke indifferently.

"As you wish, Lady Blackwood. I must take some elementary precautions to prevent your escape, however. Would you be good enough to hold out your hands?"

"Are you mad?" she asked indignantly, forgetting her pose as an invalid. She remembered just in time, and pressed her fingertips to her cheeks. "Oh, I must have misunderstood. You cannot mean to tie me up!"

"My dear Lady Blackwood, you may hold out your hands in front of you and I will tie them with this cord. Or you may resist the idea, in which case I shall send for the coachman and between us we'll truss you up like a stuffed chicken. Now, which shall it be?"

Meekly, she held out her hands. "Please leave on my gloves, my lord. It's so cold in here without a fire, and the cord chafes my wrists."

He grunted unsympathetically, but did not insist upon removing her gloves, binding the cord around her wrists with fierce efficiency. When he had finished, her hands hung uselessly in front of her, unable to grasp even medium-sized objects.

"I think that should control your adventurous spirit, Lady Blackwood. The door will be locked, of course, and bolted from outside. Please do not ruin the exquisite scrollwork by attempting to force open the door. Even if you should succeed, which I do not believe is possible, there is a servant posted outside the door to ensure that you do not proceed down the corridor. I shall leave you for a couple of hours while I eat dinner. Use the time to reflect upon your situation. Once you have signed the papers it will be my pleasure to bring you some refreshments." His glance travelled lightly around the room. "I regret that my housekeeper has neglected to provide this room with a carafe of water. I do hope that you are not too thirsty. I am sure you remember from your last visit to us that thirst is a more terrible companion than hunger."

She would not let him see how she shivered inwardly at the memory of her last imprisonment. "My uncle, the Reverend Charles Beaufort, was a very simple man," she said. "He believed passionately that good triumphs over evil and that in the end we are rewarded for our acts of kindness and punished for our deliberate cruelty. I would not like to face up to *your* reckoning, Baron Tynsdale."

He laughed easily. "It is fortunate, perhaps, that I do not share your uncle's simple philosophy. My own is more complex. However, I recommend that you do not waste these next two hours in philosophical and theological reflection, Lady Blackwood. I am not noted for my patience."

The gilt-painted door shut firmly behind him, and an iron key grated in the lock. Sarah was left alone in the cold room, its darkness relieved only by the feeble flame of one tallow candle.

FIFTEEN

Viscount Blackwood struggled to conceal his irritation. He had no desire whatsoever to be sitting in Lady Angela's pink boudoir. The afternoon was drawing to a close and he was anxious to return to his own house, ready to enjoy a quiet evening with Sarah. Perhaps if they settled down together to a comfortable family dinner they would be able to resolve the many issues still hanging between them. Moodily, he sipped at a glass of champagne, sniffing it suspiciously. Even Lady Angela's crystal seemed to smell of *Nuit d'Amour* this afternoon. He looked up, scarcely managing to hide his vexation as Lady Angela drifted into the room. Her luscious pink-and-white body was veiled in floating layers of semi-transparent silk chiffon. The Viscount found himself wondering cynically whether he had already paid for this exotic creation, or whether that treat was still in store for him.

Impatiently, he got to his feet. "Angela, I am pressed for time this evening. I responded promptly to your note, since you told me that you were in urgent need of my advice. Could you tell me how I may help you?"

With the greatest difficulty, he restrained the impulse to glance at the fob-watch hanging at his waist. "Angela, my dear, we have enjoyed so many hours in each other's company that I am loath to appear discourteous. But my presence is required elsewhere."

"With your wife, I suppose." The acrid words tumbled out before she could bite them back, but she recovered herself instantly, and glided across the floor to him, her arms opening in a ready embrace. "Everett," she pouted prettily, "I wrote to you for a good reason, but cannot we take the time to enjoy ourselves for a few minutes before I trouble you with my problems?"

The Viscount pressed a dutiful kiss on her painted cheek, but disengaged himself as soon as he could.

"I have decided that married men have little time for enjoyment," he said lightly. "My days have been so fully occupied with visits from my lawyer and my man-of-affairs, that I am considering hiding myself in the country where they cannot find me. What is your problem, Angela? If you find yourself temporarily embarrassed for funds, I should be happy to fill the gap until Lord Ross is free to attend to these matters for you."

"No," she said abruptly. "I do not want money. I need your advice as to what I should do about some documents which I have been asked to deal with." She cast one further look at the Viscount and said, almost pleadingly.

"Everett, could we not eat dinner together, as we did in the old days, before you were married?"

He did not answer her question, but turned away with ill-concealed impatience, and she sighed. Walking towards the door, she stopped by the table that held the bottle of champagne and poured out two glasses.

"I will go and get the papers from my desk, Everett. But first will you not at least join me in a glass of champagne?"

He nodded, unwilling to thwart her in this small request, and joined her at the table. She lifted her glass in a silent salute, draining the contents at a single gulp. The Viscount laughed.

"Come, come, Angela! That's no way to treat champagne! You would give more time to a glass of medicine."

"I shall watch you drink yours, my lord. I am scarcely in the mood for sipping wine."

He complied by taking another sip, and a momentary frown creased his brow. He said nothing, however, simply walking over to the window and staring down on to the darkening street. He drew the curtains with a swift movement, sending the room into semi-darkness, then walked back to Lady Angela, draining the last of his champagne as he reached her side.

"It is cosier with the curtains drawn; these March evenings can be gloomy. Now, my lady, I have to ask you for those papers. Or else I shall be forced to leave you without offering my advice. It is already dark, and I am overdue at my next appointment."

She walked hurriedly across to the door. "I will not keep you waiting, my lord. Why do you not sit by the fire in that comfortable chair, and I will rejoin you immediately."

He paced restlessly round the room once or twice, but soon sank into the winged armchair. The heat of the fire was overpowering in this place and his eyelids seemed to grow heavy. When Lady Angela returned to the room, she found the Viscount deeply asleep, his head lolling forward on his chest in ungainly abandon.

She crept over to his side and touched his hand. The sleeping Viscount did not stir. More daring now, she touched his cheek, flicking it briefly with her fingers. The Viscount remained dead to the world. As a final precaution she lifted one eyelid and was hard-pressed to contain her satisfaction when even this did not disturb the Viscount's sleep. She rose to her feet, tossing the pile of papers indifferently on to a nearby table, and turned to leave the room. Her hand was clasped in a steel grip, and her waist seized by the Viscount's strong arm.

"All right, Lady Angela. Perhaps you would be good enough to tell me why you chose to drug my champagne? It would be better, I think, if you told me the truth immediately."

"What are you talking about?" She squirmed uselessly in his iron grasp. "Everett! Let go of me! You're hurting my arm."

"And I shall probably break it if you do not stop playing me for a fool. The glass of champagne you so solicitously poured out for me is now soaking into your elegant curtains

You are dealing with a former member of the Hell Fire Club, my dear. I wasted a great deal of my youthful energies playing the fool, Angela, and I necessarily learned several tricks to aid my survival. I was rendered unconscious by a stiff dose of laudanum tipped into my wine when I was about nineteen, and that trick has not been played on me successfully since. You surely could not hope to mask the bitter taste merely by adding a little champagne and dousing your glasses in perfume? Why is it so important for me to be here this evening?"

"I don't know what you mean," she said sulkily. "You fell asleep in the chair by the fire, and now you wish to make a great mystery out of nothing. Why should I want you sleeping here in my armchair?"

The Viscount spoke slowly. "There seems little reason. But perhaps you do not want me here, particularly, you simply don't wish me to be somewhere else. Why, Angela? Why must I be kept under your eye?"

She twisted in his arms, her eyes blazing with sudden fury. "There is no reason that I know of, my lord. What do I care if you are bewitched by that skinny wife of yours—a mere child whom you dragged out from nowhere, just to insult me? I shall be better off with Lord Ross. At least he knows how to treat me, even if he is too old to be much of a lover." She tossed her head angrily. "You are here because Baron Tynsdale asked me to keep you in my house tonight. Ask *him* if you want to know why it was necessary. I was happy to do him the favour."

He released her so suddenly that she almost fell. He picked up his coat, shrugging into its tightly-fitting sleeves with the ease of long habit.

"Good-bye, Lady Angela. Please do not ring for somebody to show me out, I know my own way." He paused, still on the brink of anger, then lifted his shoulders indifferently. "Enjoy yourself in Italy, my dear. With your colouring, I prophesy that you will be all the rage within a month of your arrival."

She did not answer, but flounced over to the fireplace, pulling angrily at the bell to summon her maid. The Viscount shut the door softly behind him and, retrieving his hat and greatcoat from their resting place in the hall, stepped out quickly into the cool March evening. There seemed no reason to look back. Lady Angela belonged to his past.

"What do you mean, you don't know where Lady Blackwood is?" asked the Viscount irascibly. He tried unsuccessfully to control a mounting sensation of fear. "Did she not leave a message for me, or indicate in some other way when she might be returning.?"

Potter's expression remained studiously blank. "As I told your lordship already, her ladyship returned from a shopping expedition with Lady Sutton, and indicated to me that she would take dinner in her room." He coughed delicately. "I apprehend that her ladyship was somewhat disappointed to find you gone from home, my lord. However, before her ladyship could retire to her bedchamber, a message was delivered to her. She went out immediately, my lord, and said that she would probably be back before long. That was two hours ago, my lord. Her ladyship has not yet returned."

"Who sent the message? If you do not know, go and find out who delivered the note. Which carriage did the Viscountess order?"

"Her ladyship refused a carriage, my lord. Nor would she allow me to send for a hackney carriage, nor even a sedan chair. She walked, my lord."

"Stop looking so damned disapproving, Potter, and find out who sent that message. And send in a bottle of burgundy for me."

"Yes, my lord."

The Viscount paced restlessly up and down the long library, his thoughts racing in increasingly narrow circles and his feelings prey to a growing conviction that by the time he found Sarah it might be too late. Too late for what, his tired brain refused to specify. The sounds of a violent altercation finally penetrated the combined barriers of thick stone walls and his own chaotic thoughts. He flung open the door to find a dishevelled Potter attempting to bar the entrance to the library against a struggling Aggie Meadows. She, in turn, was obviously using all her resources, physical and vocal, in order to gain admission to the Viscount's presence. The servants' battle ceased at the sight of the Viscount, both of them tumbling into immediate and slightly incoherent explanations.

"Be silent!" roared the Viscount in exasperation. "Potter, I should be obliged if you would find out the answer to the question which I asked earlier. Aggie, what is the problem? You cannot brawl with the butler in the front hall, you know, even if you are a special favourite of the Viscountess."

Aggie bobbed an apologetic curtsey. Now that she had the Viscount's attention, she seemed willing to return to her usual docile manner. But the tongue-tied silence she had always maintained in front of the Viscount vanished as soon as the butler disappeared round a bend in the corridor.

"My lord, I must talk to you," she said agitatedly, the words tumbling out in her eagerness to speak. "I just got back from the Dowager Viscountess's house, and my Jem was here, waiting to speak to me. He's been up to Greenside, and he says it's right terrible up there. Everybody knows the Baron is run off his legs, and not a drop of money going into the estate. Not a repair been made nor a crop planted since the old Baron died. The bailiff was turned off, and the new one sent out a whole gang of riff-raff searching the countryside for my Miss Sarah and Miss Cassie. And now she's gone." The old woman's voice was drowned in strangled sobs and the silent tears coursed down her cheeks.

"Every time I leave 'er alone, something happens to 'er. I *old* 'er it must be the Baron what stole her away last time, but she wouldn't listen. And as soon as my back's turned, he gets my Miss Sarah again." In her distress, Aggie reached out and pulled at the Viscount's sleeve. "You will get her back, won't you my lord? You won't let the Baron make away with her? If you talk to Jem, he knows all the Baron's houses. Last time, the Baron wanted 'er to sign some papers, although of course we didn't know 'twas the Baron on account of he kept her blindfold. Mebbe there's still time to get her back, if she 'as the commonsense not to sign nothing."

The Viscount gently pushed the old housekeeper down on to a chair in front of the fire, motioning her to silence.

"Aggie, you must calm down. Who is Jem, and why was he at Greenside? I gather that you are talking of Baron Tynsdale, but why should you believe he has taken my wife? And what do you mean about 'last time'? You had better explain everything to me, Aggie, or I cannot decide if Sarah is truly in danger."

The housekeeper smoothed her apron with trembling hands. "I'll try and explain it again, my lord. Jem is my brother. He used to be groom for Miss Sarah's father, and he come with us to London when the girls moved from Hampshire with the Reverend Charles. After those villains run off with 'er, and after you brought 'er back to this 'ouse, Miss Sarah agreed that Jem should go and ferret around a bit at Greenside, to see what was going on there. I told 'er she *had* to do something after somebody kidnapped her and tried to drown her in the river. And it seemed only right to start with 'er own family."

"But what are you saying? Surely the Viscountess . . . That is to say, I believed that Lady Blackwood had attempted to end her own life. Are you telling me that somebody tried to murder her?"

Aggie sounded impatient. "Of course somebody tried to kill 'er, although she wouldn't let me tell you about it. Why should Miss Sarah try to do away with 'erself? Full of spunk she is, and all set up to go as a governess at that school in

Cheltenham. I did tell 'er she wouldn't find being a teacher all that special, but she'd set her heart on it. Said it would be 'er first real taste of independence. Miss Sarah was always a clever one, and her old schoolmistress jumped at the chance to take her back as a teacher once the Reverend Charles was dead.''

"I did not realize that Sarah was so well-prepared to face her future. But if her employment was to be in Cheltenham, why was she remaining in London in such uncomfortable circumstances?''

"Miss Sarah wouldn't leave town until I was fixed up with a new job, so I was out every day trying to find another decent place to work. But you're right, it was a terrible part of town for her to live in, and that curate of her sister's no more use than a babe—and not half as responsible. 'Twas hardly dark when I got back to the vicarage on the night somebody kidnapped Miss Sarah, but there wasn't a sign of 'er, and the curate off somewhere in the parish visiting. He had a meeting or a committee for every night of the week, that man.''

The Viscount spared a moment of sympathy for the poor curate, who had obviously failed to live up to the high standards set by the Reverend Charles. "But why do you believe Sarah was kidnapped?" he asked abruptly. "Forgive me, but how caan you be sure that she was not overcome by thoughts of the lonely prospect ahead of her?''

Aggie looked at him pityingly. "All the chairs were pulled over in the front parlour. I knew she'd never have gone out at night without me, not after Miss Cassie died, so I knew there was something wrong. Took me hours to get the place straight, that night. But I never knew what had 'appened to my Miss Sarah until a servant came and brought me round 'ere. That was nearly a week after she'd gone from the 'ouse, and no news about her from nobody. It was as if the ground 'ad opened and swallowed 'er up. Half out of my mind with worry I was, my lord, and that's a fact. *She* told me what had 'appened to her, my lord, which is how I know she was kidnapped. Two men came and took her out of the vicarage, and she was kept locked up in a room with her eyes covered. No food, one glass of water a day, which is why she seemed near starving when you found her. Only one person came near her all the time she was locked up, and it wasn't one of the men what kidnapped her. It was a gentleman who kept nagging her to sign some papers. She never would sign them, of course. She knew he was a gentleman by the way he talked, but she never saw his face on account of the blind-fold."

"That is a frightening story, Aggie," said the Viscount slowly. "Have you any idea what this gentleman wished your mistress to sign? And why do you think he changed his mind and had her thrown into the river?"

Aggie sniffed scornfully. "He knew the Beauforts were gentry, my lord, even if they weren't wealthy enough to satisfy old Baron Tynsdale. I reckon he only waited to make sure none of her Beaufort relatives were making a fuss over 'er being missing, and then he didn't bother no more about signing papers. Just had her tossed into the water. He wasn' to know that she could swim. After all, there aren't many young girls as can. Nasty, heathenish thing to do, if you ask me. But Miss Sarah learned when her mother went to the seacoast at Brighton. I never thought I'd be grateful to that new-fangled doctor who recommended sea-bathing for her mama's consumption. But it saved Miss Sarah's life, and that's a fact."

"But why did she not explain all this to me? We could have pursued a proper investigation with all the resources I have to command. Then the people responsible could have been brought to book."

Aggie looked at the Viscount shrewdly. "She was in two minds about you, my lord. She wanted to believe you, but for all she knew different, you might have been the murderer!"

"But that is quite ridiculous!" exclaimed the Viscount

impatiently. "How could she had considered such an idea?"

Aggie shrugged. "It's not so stupid, my lord. Why else was you wandering around a workhouse fever ward, unless it was to find somebody special—and for a reason you couldn't broadcast to the world? Viscounts don't go wedding women out of the poorhouse, anybody knows that."

The Viscount ran impatient fingers through his hair, and then spoke grimly. "My selfish desire not to be shown in a bad light seems to have had disastrous consequences. I had better explain to you something of what I was doing. For . . . personal . . . reasons, I wished to become a widower. I went to the workhouse simply because it was close at hand and likely to be a place where I could find a dying woman. It was sheer chance that I selected Sarah for my bride. Any other woman close to death would have done equally as well."

As he spoke, he wondered if the words were wholly true. Even in the dark corner of the fever ward, Sarah's ethereal beauty had drawn him like a magnet. Determinedly, he brushed aside such speculations. There was no time for contemplating the vagaries of fate while Sarah remained lost to him. A sudden panic seized him, a gaping fear as he faced the prospect of a life made suddenly empty without the tantalizing glimpse of Sarah's smile, the sound of her soft voice or the feel of her slim body pressed against his own. With a sharp gesture of his hand, he cut off his thoughts and dismissed the objections forming on Aggie's lips.

"No. There is no time to explain further. You must trust me."

Aggie spoke slowly. "I do trust you, my lord, although I don't altogether know why. 'Tis certain that you've dazzled my poor Miss Sarah. Jem will help us to track her down, my lord. But we need horses, fast ones, my lord, and the money to hire fresh ones when the first lot get tired."

The Viscount pulled at the bell-rope. "Get Jem," he said curtly to Aggie as he waited for a footman to answer the summons. "I shall drive my racing curricle. He will have to ride in place of my tiger."

"He's waiting in the stables, my lord. I'll fetch 'im round to the front of the house. He knows about horses, and he's strong, my lord. And he thinks he knows where the Baron will have taken her ladyship."

It was Potter himself who answered the Viscount's summons, glancing at Aggie with stately dislike as she scurried hastily from the Viscount's presence.

"I need my driving coat, Potter," said the Viscount. "Don't go yourself, send one of the footmen to fetch it. I want to know what you have discovered about the letter which was delivered to the Viscountess."

"It was brought to the back door by one of the corner crossing-sweepers, my lord. I sent one of the footmen to find the lad, and he's waiting in the kitchen if you should care to speak to him." The butler hesitated, before adding carefully. "The lad is a very *ignorant* type of person, my lord. I could talk to him myself and then send him about his business if you would prefer not to talk to him."

"Bring him in here," said the Viscount decisively. "And hurry them with my curricle, will you please, Potter?"

The crossing-sweeper crept gingerly into the library behind a supercilious footman. A dirty and undernourished boy of some ten years old, he was probably as ignorant as Potter claimed. A life so far filled exclusively with the urgent necessity of procuring his next meal had not left him with overmuch time for worrying about the advantages of intellectual enrichment. However, his native intelligence was high, and his curiosity had been piqued by the succession of events which had marked this particular day. His blue eyes, gleaming cheekily in the scruffy pallor of his face, looked up at the Viscount with considerable satisfaction.

"Bang-up place you've got 'ere, guv'nor," he remarked cheerfully. "Never seen nuffin' like it, in all me born days."

"I'm gratified that it meet with your approval," said the

Viscount dryly. He looked at the thin face and intelligent eyes, then turned away abruptly. "Did they give you something to eat in the kitchens?"

"Eel pie and a plate of cold giblets," said the crossing sweeper with evident satisfaction. "And one of the women said I could 'ave a bowl of mutton broth if I answered you proper."

"You certainly may. But do not think you must invent answers to my questions just to get the broth. I am trying to find someone who is . . . lost . . . and you may be able to help me if you answer truthfully. If you cannot answer my questions, just say so. I promise that you shall still have your soup." He looked searchingly at the urchin. "Who gave you the letter that you delivered here earlier this evening?"

"It was an ordinary type of cove, not a real gentleman, but dressed warm and tidy. I see a carriage waiting on the corner of the mews, and I did think mebbe he was the coachman, 'cept he wasn't wearing no livery. This cove gave me a groat to take a note to this 'ouse. Said it was a love letter for one of the serving-girls. I give the piece of paper to one of the nobs in your kitchen, and I saw a woman come out of the 'ouse not fifteen minutes later, so I thought everything was all right. I never saw who she met, because the carriage 'ad moved away, round the corner like. But I 'eard it drive off, so I reckoned she must 'ave met up with 'er lover. Smashing looker she was, dressed like a real lady with a fancy coat and fur muff." He looked anxiously at the Viscount. "I 'ope I done right, sir. Fourpence is a lot o' money for me, but I wouldn't 'ave delivered the note if I'd known I was doin' wrong."

"There is no reason for you to feel guilty. If you can remember nothing else about the man who gave you the letter, I will ring for a footman to show you the way back into the kitchen, so that you may have your broth. You did not happen to observe in which direction the carriage drove off?"

"Well, it didn't come back past me, guv'nor. So it must

'ave gone south or west. And now I come to think about it, the wheels made such a racket is must 'ave driven off at a spanking old pace."

"Thank you. What is your name?"

"Daniel, sir."

"Well, Daniel, your information has been very helpful. Here is the footman come to take you back to the kitchen, and I hope to bring me word that my curricle is ready."

The footman seemed reluctant to speak in the presence of such a disreputable urchin, but he condescended to incline his head in acknowledgment of the Viscount's question.

"Your curricle is at the door, my lord. The stable-hand is walking the horses so that they will not take chill."

The Viscount walked swiftly into the hall, snatching up a riding crop and gloves from the waiting Potter. "Daniel has been of considerable assistance to me. Make sure that he is given the soup he was promised, and a shilling to make up for the time he has lost on the job."

The footman looked at Daniel distastefully. "Yes, my lord, I will see to it."

But he spoke to the empty air, for the Viscount, pushing his arms into his greatcoat, was already running down the steps and out into the waiting curricle. He halted only when Aggie came puffing round from the back of the house.

"My lord!" she called out. "One of the kitchen lads found this note pushed under the back door. It's addressed to you, my lord. Perhaps it's from Miss Sarah!"

The Viscount snatched the note with eager hands, ripping open the thin wax seal and scanning the closely written words. The lines of his face hardened into an expression of disgust, and he flung the reins back into Jem's keeping.

"You may stable the horses," he said curtly. "I shall not be needing them after all."

"What . . . what is it, my lord?" asked Aggie timidly. The forbidding scowl on the Viscount's forehead did not invite questions. He looked at the old servant briefly, before tossing her the letter.

"You may read it," he said. "It seems neither of us was fully in my wife's confidence."

Aggie read the letter with painful concentration, running after the Viscount to clutch at the sweeping capes of his coat. "No, my lord! Don't go back inside. You must not believe it! It's the work of a villain. Miss Sarah never had so much as a friend that I didn't know about, leave alone a lover. She hasn't run off with anybody, my lord. You must believe me." She wrung her hands together in a desperate gesture of supplication "It's a trick, my lord, to make sure you don't chase after her until that wicked man has got what he wants from her. Never believe that she'd betray your trust, my lord. She's crazy for you, eating her heart out for your attention, and that's a fact."

The Viscount slowed to an uncertain stop. "But even the crossing-sweeper thought he was delivering a love-letter. And he said she went quite willingly to the assignation. If only we knew one another better!" The exclamation was made almost to himself. Reluctantly, he turned round and called back the departing Jem.

"Very well, Aggie. I'll take your word for it that the letter is a forgery. If the Baron is as unscrupulous as you believe him to be, I suppose a forged letter would rank low on his list of iniquities." He sprang up on the driving seat and accepted the reins from a stable-boy. "Where shall we go, Jem? Your sister thinks that you can assist me to trace my wife."

"Aye." Jem's voice still retained the soft burr of the Hampshire countryside. "I checked the Baron's town house already, my lord, and he isn't there. The only other place he's got close enough to town is a little property in Streatham. He inherited it from his mother and keeps it up as a country retreat when he wants to get away from town for a few days. I know exactly where it is, and I reckon it would be perfect for keeping somebody prisoner. And near enough for the Baron to come back to town every day, if he doesn't mind a bit of rough riding. It's only eight miles from town."

"So we shall try the Streatham house first. Fortunately, it's a good road and a fair night. We may be there within the hour. Stand back from their heads, Aggie! I'm letting them go!"

Aggie crouched back against the railings, and watched the curricle speed into the distance. Now there was nothing to do except wait—and hope. She sighed. She seemed to have been doing a great deal of hoping these past few weeks.

SIXTEEN

Baron Tynsdale of Greenside welcomed the Viscount into his small drawing-room with every appearance of delight.

"My dear sir, this is an unexpected pleasure! If you have not dined, may I offer you some refreshment? I always bring my chef out from town with me, so you need not fear you will be subjected to a gastronomic horror."

"No, thank you. I did not come here upon a social visit."

"But my dear friend—we are such old acquaintances that I feel I should claim you as a friend, do you not agree?—I did not for one moment imagine that you had driven all the way from town merely to engage in the exchange of social pleasantries. But surely your business, whatever it is, can be better discussed over a glass of wine and a few choice dishes of food?"

"I think not, Tynsdale. I have come about my wife."

"Ah yes! The lovely Viscountess. But please, I must insist that you sit down." The Baron disposed himself on an elaborately embroidered chair, and appeared to lose himself in the contemplation of a Fragonard portrait which hung over the mantelpiece. "Exquisite piece of work, is it not? It reminds me a little of your dear Viscountess our . . . er . . . mutual kinswoman."

"So you do know," said the Viscount, without turning to look at the painting.

"How could you doubt it, my dear fellow? I imagine that the Viscountess's startling resemblance to her late mother will ultimately jog quite a few memories among our acquaintance in the *haut ton*. But I am quite prepared to acknowledge the relationship long before tongues begin to wag. There was really no need for you to come scrambling out of town just to reassure yourself upon so minor a point. I imagine that *was* why you decided to . . . ah . . . pursue me to this country cottage?"

"Streatham is less than eight miles from Mount Street, Tynsdale. That hardly constitutes a journey from Land's End, you know. However, I have not come to discuss my wife's connection to your family. I have come to ask your assistance in helping to find out where she is."

The Baron's expression hardened immediately, but his voice remained bantering. "My imagination quivers with questions as to how you came to lose her, my lord. But I assure you, I am the last person to have any special knowledge of her whereabouts. As you must know, contact between your bride and my family has been non-existent. Until the ball given by your mother, the Dowager Viscountess, I had not even had the pleasure of meeting my cousin."

The Viscount rose to his feet and paced restlessly about the room. "We can fence, Tynsdale, all night and eventually I shall be constrained to come out and say what I think. I believe that my wife has been abducted, and that you are holding her here against her will—as you did once before."

The Baron looked distinctly ruffled. "My lord, I will make every possible allowance for one who must be suffering under considerable anguish of mind. However, you know that I cannot allow you to make such accusations and leave them to pass unchallenged. I ask you to accept my sympathy in your unpleasant task, but I must also ask you to leave. I understand the urgency of your mission and why you feel that you do not have time to dally taking refreshment."

The Viscount laughed softly. "A worthy try, Tynsdale, but such bluster will not suffice, I am afraid. I am going to search this house for my wife, and if I cannot search it with your permission, I shall do it without."

"You are very bold, my lord. I am amazed that you would take such risks with an outright villain like myself. Are you not afraid that I shall summon my servants and have you done away with right here on the middle of the drawing-room carpet?"

"No," said the Viscount softly, completely ignoring the heavy sarcasm of the Baron's questions. "There are two very good reasons why I shall be allowed to leave this house unharmed. The first reason is that my groom remains outside, hidden from your servants and heavily armed, of course. He knows exactly why I am here, and if I do not return within the next fifteen minutes or so, he will ride back to the Golden Sun Inn where I have several local labourers just waiting to come and find me. Secondly, whatever your plans were, they have not succeeded. But if you retain any hope of getting out of this scandal alive and with sufficient reputation left to make existence in the civilized world tolerable, then you need my goodwill in hushing the matter up. Are you prepared to take me to my wife now, Baron Tynsdale?"

The Baron walked slowly towards a console table at the side of the room. "You do not seem to leave me much choice," he said.

"Even less than you imagine," said the Viscount slowly. "I should not try to open that desk drawer if I were you, for if you turn round you will see that I am holding a pistol and it is aimed in your direction." He smiled apologetically. "It has a hair trigger, you know, and I should not like my hand to tremble."

The Baron shrugged. "You may go where you please, my lord. I imagine you do not require my escort?"

"I think, on the whole, that I should feel safer to have you in front of me rather than at my back. Perhaps you would pick up an extra candle in case the servants have not yet lit the lamps in the upstairs rooms?"

The Baron picked up a small candelabra and walked out of the drawing-room in grim silence. The Viscount walked steadily behind him, flinging open the doors of the empty rooms and calling out Sarah's name. He would not allow himself to think of the consequences if Sarah could not be found, or how he would apologize to the Baron if his suspicions should prove to be unfounded. The Baron walked in the direction of the green baize service door and quickly the Viscount called him back.

"I think we will check the bedrooms before venturing into your kitchens," he said. "Perhaps you would be good enough to lead the way."

The Viscount sensed the moment of hesitation in the Baron's manner and he felt a flash of triumph that his façade of calm condescension had finally been pierced. There was no doubt that Baron Tynsdale's footsteps slowly involuntarily as they neared the upper floor of the house. The corridor upstairs was brilliantly lit, but most of the rooms lay in shadow. The Viscount went from one bedchamber to the next, calling Sarah's name and listening for any sound, however slight, which would indicate her presence in the darkened rooms. Most of the doors were unlocked, but they finally reached a dim corner where they found a burly manservant standing propped against the lintels of an elegant powder-blue door.

The servant straightened as his master approached, but whatever words he had meant to speak faded into silence as a gleam of candle-light fell on the pearl handle of the Viscount's pistol. The Viscount gestured to the servant. "Stand next to your master. And keep your hands in front of you." He reached for the doorknob even as the servant lumbered to the Baron's side, twisting it with mounting fury as it failed to give under the pressure of his hands.

"Sarah!" he called out. "Stand away from the door. I shall be with you in a moment." There was no sound from inside, but he was sure he had reached his objective, and he seethed silently at the thought of Sarah—his wife—bound and gagged, unable to respond to him.

"You may unlock this door," he said to the Baron, "or I shall kick it down. And if that proves too difficult to do, remember that I shall shortly have several stalwart labourers arriving to help me in my task."

"I do not have the key," hissed the Baron. "This room has never been used since my mother died. You may try to kick it down if you wish."

"I am becoming angry," said the Viscount conversationally. "And when I am angry, my hand trembles uncontrollably. It would be . . . distressing . . . if there should be a tragic accident here before somebody hands me the key."

The servant looked nervously at the Baron before reaching hesitantly into the pocket of his jerkin.

"This here's the key," he said gruffly. "There ain't nothin' worth getting killed over."

With slightly unsteady fingers, the Viscount fitted the key into the lock. Remembering the way Sarah had looked when he found her in the workhouse, he dreaded the sight of her pale face reduced once again to abject terror. Angrily he ordered the Baron to stand back and thrust open the door with the heel of his boot. Their candle illuminated the bare room, flickering over the undisturbed cover of the bed and the pale blue of the carpet. A faint smell of burning hung in the air, and a few ashes stirred in the draught from the newly-opened door. Otherwise the room could have been unoccupied for months as the Baron had claimed.

With an exclamation of disbelief, the Viscount thrust back the curtains of the bed and then pulled at the draperies covering the window, expecting to see Sarah's huddled form behind every fold of cloth.

"Sarah!" he yelled, rage and fright making his voice almost unrecognizable. But no answering murmur came back from the empty room. Silently, he acknowledged the truth. Sarah was not here, and he did not think she was anywhere in the house. Lost in a confusion of unhappy feelings, he failed to observe the astonished glances exchanged by the Baron and his servant. Listlessly, the Viscount waved his gun to indicate that they should precede him out of the room.

"Stay down here while I search the attics," he said savagely. He would not find Sarah up there, and he knew it, but some streak of determination forced him to carry the search through to its logical conclusion. The contents of the note, brought to him by Aggie just before he left, now came back to flood his mind with revulsion. He glanced with desultory uninterest through the servants' bedrooms and storage quarters in the attics, and then rejoined the waiting Baron filled with a corroding sensation of disillusion. The alternating hopes and fears of the evening drained him of the capacity for constructive thought, and now he could only feel sorrow for the brief glimpse of some emotion—he hesitated to call it love—which he had shared with Sarah. Even the awkwardness of his position *vis-à-vis* the Baron failed to excite any very strong emotion. He could think only of Sarah, presumably now luxuriating in the arms of her unknown lover as their carriage hurried them to a secret destination.

A convenient numbness protected him from the most acute sensations of embarrassment as he returned to face the Baron. He offered his apologies for the intrusion into the Baron's house with formal dignity, expecting—almost hoping—that the Baron would demand satisfaction for the insults offered to him. But even this relief was denied to him. Baron Tynsdale accepted his stilted words of apology with bland condescension.

"My dear Blackwood, I quite understand. Or at least, if I do not understand, I can sympathize with your present unhappy situation. Lady Blackwood is my kinswoman, even if she is not yet acknowledged as such. Let me assure you, my dear fellow, that I shall do my utmost to assist you in hushing up any . . . er . . . scandal that may result from Lady Blackwood's unexplained absence." He escorted the Viscount politely to the front door, "Pray do not let me detain you. I know you must be anxious to turn your search in another direction. Perhaps to the house of some younger man . . .?"

The Viscount gritted his teeth at the unspoken insult, springing back up on to his racing curricle in bleak silence.

"Forgive the intrusion," he said again brusquely, and then set his horses in motion with a vicious flick of the whip that was utterly out of keeping with his normal calm and expert handling. Jem clung on to his perch with silent desperation, glad that the chill night had left the road almost deserted. He would not fancy tearing through the main street of the village with the Viscount in this reckless mood.

The words of Sarah's note—there could no longer be any doubt that she was its author—drummed through the Viscount's mind in hideous rhythm with the beat of the horses' hooves. "Do not try to find me," she had written, "because we plan to leave for the Continent on the first available packet."

Briefly, he allowed himself to meditate on the falsity of women's nature, marvelling at the inborn female capacity to act out a rôle. Angela, who at last stood revealed to him in all the meanness of her mercenary nature, was the soul of honesty when compared with the false image of awakening innocence so artfully projected by Sarah. Unwillingly, his thoughts flew back to one night they had spent together, reliving the hours of passionate love-making. It was hard not to laugh out loud at the depths of his self-deception. While he had imagined that he was initiating Sarah into the delights of physical passion, in reality he himself had been subjected to expert deception at the hands of a woman already experienced in the manifold ways of pleasing a man. Deliberately he tortured himself as the horses galloped recklessly through the night. How many men had lost themselves in the enchantment of Sarah's slim body? How many men had been deceived by her soft cries of pleasure, her murmured words of shy affection? His hands tightened on the reins, jerking them back with a harsh movement, causing the horses to rear as the bits tore at the softness of their mouths.

Wearily, the Viscount allowed the reins to slacken, struggling to bring the spirited horses once again under control. He was pleased at the small tussle with the animals, almost glad to hear the frightened intake of breath from the silent Jem, perched on the back of the curricle. The need for physical action released his brain from its sickening struggle to reconcile his memories of Sarah with the harsh reality that now seemed to be taking shape around him. Angrily he concentrated his thoughts on the road ahead. There must be no more jabbing at the horses' mouths.

There was no disguising Jem's sigh of relief when the carriage plunged to a standstill outside the house in Mount Street. Torn between admiration for the incredible skill with which the Viscount had handled the reins during the latter part of the journey, and abject terror over the speed at which they had hurtled through the night, Jem was anxious to get the horses round to the stables and recapture his nerve before facing his sister with the news that Miss Sarah had not been found. Jem, of course, had no idea what the Viscount had learned at the house of Baron Tynsdale. But whatever it was, it required no genius to see that the information had been far from the Viscount's liking.

With the ease of long practice, Potter caught the gloves and riding crop hurled at him as the Viscount walked in. He watched the Viscount's angry progress into the library with secret dismay. It was one thing for his master to storm about in a rage, it was quite another for him to show such tight-lipped, harsh despair. Potter hurried into the kitchens and returned with a decanter of the best brandy and a large glass. He took it straight in to the Viscount, who poured out a generous measure and tossed it off with a rigid concentration of energy. He looked up and saw the butler watching him with worried disapproval, and a small smile twisted his lips.

"You'd better get out of here, Potter, and tell that damn valet of mine to get himself to bed. I have every intention of staying here until I'm too drunk to move. You can come in and shuffle me into bed tomorrow morning. Now get out, and don't come back in."

"Yes, my lord."

Potter closed the door quietly behind him, an apprehensive frown wrinkling his brow. Even when the old Viscount had died and the terms of his will had been made known, the new Viscount had not been this distraught. He spied Aggie Meadows, standing uncertainly in a corner of the hall, and in his anxiety, he overcame his natural reluctance to confide in an outsider.

"He's powerful upset," said Potter quietly. "Didn't say one word to me, except that I was to get out and not go back in. Whatever do you think has happened?"

Aggie shook her head in despair. "Jem says he tore out of the Baron's house like a madman. But there weren't no sign of Miss Sarah. Oh! Why doesn't he go and look for her somewhere else?" Slow tears rolled down Aggie's wrinkled cheeks. "Some ruffian 'as got her, and the Viscount isn't going to lift another finger to find her. What wouldn't I give to know what that Baron Tynsdale said to set him off the scent!"

A faint knocking at the door interrupted the servants' agitated conference. "Now who can be calling at this hour of the night?" Potter muttered as he hurried off to open the door. "Best get back to the kitchens," he said to Aggie. "Don't want to have people wondering why you're here in the hall."

Potter opened the d.or, his manner at its most magisterial. At the sight of the visitor, however, his mouth dropped open in undignified astonishment.

"My lady!" he exclaimed, and then as the full extent of her bedraggled condition dawned upon him, he exclaimed again. "Oh, my lady! Whatever has happened to you?"

Sarah walked slowly into the hall, trying to gather her torn and dirty clothes around her. Some pieces of grass clung to the hem of her gown, and her eyes were brusied with fatigue.

"The Viscount," she said unsteadily. "Where is he? I must talk to him."

Aggie ran forward from the corner of the hall, and rested a proprietorial arm around her mistress. "First you're going to bed, my lady. and then you can do your talking."

"No," said Sarah obstinately, although she swayed as she tried to stand alone. "I must . . . see . . . the Viscount. It's time I told him the truth. I was blind—foolish beyond belief—not to realize that it was Baron Tynsdale who kidnapped me before."

Potter made a warning gesture to Aggie behind Sarah's back, and Aggie subsided into an uncertain silence.

"The Viscount is in the library, my lady," said the butler formally. "If you would care to join him there I will bring you some refreshment. Some tea, perhaps, and some bread and butter?"

"Thank you." Sarah smiled at him gratefully. "Go upstairs, Aggie I will talk to you later."

Potter rapped gently at the library door. It had not been more than half an hour since he left the Viscount alone with the brandy, but at the rate his master had started to consume the spirits, it was not difficult to guess what sort of a scene might meet the Viscountess's eye.

There was no reply from within the library, and gingerly he pushed open the door. The Viscount was sprawled in the old armchair at the side of the fireplace. His cravat hung loosely around his neck, and the once-full decanter of brandy was almost empty. He held his hands cupped round the bowl of the brandy glass, and stared broodingly into the depths of the fire.

He heard the creak of the door as it opened, and he spoke without looking up from his contemplation of the flickering tongues of flame.

"Get out!" he said briefly, without inflection.

Potter moved hesitantly into the room, uncertain how he should attract his master's attention.

"I said you were to get out, and stay out."

Sarah walked forward into the candlelight, and Potter faded tactfully from the room.

"Everett," she said softly. "I have come back."

"*Sarah!*" The Viscount sprang to his feet and strode across the room to her side. "Sarah!" he said again, as he crushed her against his body, wrapping her in his arms as if he could not fully believe the reality of her presence.

She swayed against him, exhaustion and hunger forgotten as she received his kisses with passionate abandon. Her lips trembled softly against his face, and her long lashes closed in a dark sweep across her cheeks.

Suddenly he pushed her away from him, thrusting his hands through his hair, then crossing the room as if to put as much physical space between them as possible.

"Why have you come back?" he asked cynically, although his voice was not yet entirely steady. "Has your lover abandoned you already?" Cruelly, his eyes raked her dishevelled form. "Lud! You do not seem to have played your cards very intelligently, my dear. You look as if you have had an . . . arduous . . . journey back to my house."

"Everett," she said, in a voice made colourless by fatigue, "I am too tired to unravel your mysteries now. Do you not wish to hear what has happened to me? I thought . . ." Her voice broke on a small, smothered sob, "For a moment, I thought that you were as pleased to see me back as I was to be here."

"Very affecting, madam. But even your skills as an actress, great thought they are, cannot quite persuade me to forget the graphic descriptions contained in your letter of farewell. You cannot write in the afternoon that you are going to join your lover, and then expect your husband to receive you with courteous smiles and warm embraces when you return in the evening."

"I see. The Baron has been even cleverer than I feared," said Sarah quietly. "It would be useless to protest that I have no knowledge of the letter you speak of, I suppose?"

The Viscount was saved the necessity of replying by the entrance of Potter, carrying a large silver tray, amply spread with a tea service, cups and two tempting plates of thin bread and tiny cakes. He placed the tray on a low table, and smiled at Sarah with warm approbation.

"You must sit down, my lady. If you will pardon the liberty, I must say that you appear quite done in. The tea will refresh you, my lady. And Mrs. Meadows is waiting for you upstairs, whenever you wish to retire." He smiled at her again, resisting the urge to place an avuncular and reassuring arm around her fragile shoulders, and once again withdrew discreetly from the room.

The Viscount laughed harshly, goading hiself to attack and cover the pity he felt welling up inside him. "I am amazed you had so little success with your lover. If you can even wrap Potter around your thumb, I would have though no ordinary man could fail to be enslaved for ever."

"There was no lover," said Sarah listlessly. "Would you care for some tea, my lord? Perhaps you might care to hear my story, even though you are determined not to believe me." Her voice broke on a small attempt at a laugh. "I suppose you are not planning to cast me from the house precisely at this moment?"

She reached out her hand to offer the cup of tea, but as the Viscount came over to take it from her, her hand wavered in an erratic pattern, spilling the tea down the side of her dress and on to the priceless Aubusson carpet.

"Forgive me, my lord," she whispered weakly, and crumpled into an unconscious huddle on the arm of the chair.

With a few swift steps, the Viscount was at her side, resting her head against his arms, and murmuring words of endearment into her hair.

"Sarah, I'm sorry. I didn't mean it. Can you not see that I'm half out of my mind with jealousy? I have worried so much as to where you might be." He smoothed the hair out of her eyes, watching the desperate pallor of her face, and reached for her wrists, anxious to chafe her cold hands back to some semblance of warmth and life.

As he touched her wrists, he felt a stickiness beneath the soft frills of her sleeves and, overcome by a sudden fear, he pushed back the thin fabric of her gown. The raw, burnt flesh of his wife's hands lay exposed to his gaze, the remnants of cord still bound and knotted around her wrists. In silent horror he ran to the door, calling out for Potter as he went.

"Oh my Gawd!" For once, Potter's habitual dignity entirely deserted him when he saw the state of Sarah's hands, and he struggled visibly to regain his composure as the Viscount barked out his orders.

"Get the Meadows woman in here right away! And see that she comes with water and clean dressings. Send one of the stable-hands to fetch Dr. Thompson. Make sure that the doctor realizes this is urgent. That he must come at once." He held some of the rapidly cooling tea to Sarah's lips. "Come, Sarah," he said gently. "You must try and drink. You will feel better once you have taken something."

He held the liquid against her lips, remembering the other occasion on which he had tried to force life back into her unconscious body. The sights and smells of the workhouse seemed to rise up to choke him, and he had to struggle to put the vivid imagines out of his mind. Tenderly, he trickled the liquid down her throat, sighing with relief when her eyes opened and looked at him with full recognition.

"The Baron," she said urgently. "It was the Baron who took me. This time *and* before, when they tried to drown me in the river."

"I understand," said the Viscount. "Here. You must drink some more tea and not try to talk any more. Aggie is coming to tend to your wrists and help you upstairs to bed." For a moment his expression hardened into its previous lines of uncompromising fury. "How did it happen, Sarah? Did the Baron do that to your hands?"

"No." She tried to keep her voice light. "I did it to myself. The Baron tied my hands so that I would not be able to escape. But he left me one candle—there was a document he wanted me to read—so I burned through the cord he had used to tie me. It caught fire, and for a few minutes I could not control the flames. But once my hands were free of the bonds, it was simple to extinguish the flames, and quite easy to climb out of the window. The house is old, and there was no glass, only wooden shutters which were bolted on the inside." A faint smile lit up the exhaustion of her face. "The Baron clearly did not expect me to go adventuring, for the windows were not barred and it was not difficult to climb out of my prison. I pushed the casements shut behind me, since I hoped to delay the Baron's pursuit long enough to run down to the village. There was a horse-chestnut tree growing right up against the house, just waiting for somebody to climb down it. But I suppose the Baron felt quite safe once he had tied me up. It would have been impossible to climb down the tree with my hands bound against my body." She laughed a little tremulously. "It was not *quite* as easy as I'd hoped, even with my hands untied. But it is amazing how panic lends a spur to one's heels."

Silently, the Viscount raised her hands and examined the broken finger-nails and cut flesh of her palms. His lips tightened, but he said nothing about her story.

"Don't talk any more," he ordered. "You must rest. Here is Aggie, who has come to take care of you. When you have slept, you can tell us how you managed to get back from Streatham."

A ghost of a smile hovered around Sarah's mouth. "I walked back from Streatham, my lord. Seven miles is nothing to a country parson's daughter."

An indefinable expression flickered across the Viscount's stern features, but again he said nothing. He raised her injured hands to his lips and gently pressed a kiss against the finger-tips.

"I have to go out, Sarah, but Aggie will look after you and Jem shall spend the night outside your bedroom door. You have nothing to fear, my dear. Only Dr. Thompson will be admitted by the servants. You may rest easily, Sarah."

"I wish you would stay." In her weakness, she could not avoid letting the words escape.

His arm rested lightly on her shoulders, and he kissed her hand again, oblivious to the presence of the servants.

"I would like to stay with you, Sarah, but I cannot. There are . . . pressing matters . . . which require my presence elsewhere. The entire household is at your service, my dear. Do not hesitate to command whatever you need."

"Thank you." She turned her face away, so that he would not see the hint of sadness she could not conceal. The Viscount was kind to her, and undoubtedly sorry that she had been hurt, but not enough to cancel his pressing engagements. She thought of Lady Angela Thorpe, pink and opulent as she had been at the ball. There was no hope of competing with such expert voluptuousness, and she almost wished that she had never been informed of Lady Angela's rôle in the Viscount's life. She could not suppress a quick sigh. Perhaps one day there would be children to care for, sons and daughters of the Viscount on whom she could expend her deep store of love.

She could not lose herself in these mournful reflections for long. She could sense the Viscount's impatience to be gone and Aggie descended on her in a swirl of clucks and exclamations of concern. Sarah smiled wanly, too exhausted to protest at Aggie's determined cosseting. She was glad when the Viscount made a move to leave almost as soon as Aggie started to dress her hands. She felt in danger of fainting again, and had no wish to exhibit such weakness in front of her husband. The Viscount cast her one final searching glance before bowing politely from the doorway.

"I know that I relinquish you to good hands. I am sorry that I am . . . forced . . . to leave you. Take great care of her,

Aggie. I shall see you, Sarah, first thing in the morning, when I can be sure you are rested."

She tried to ignore the agony of Aggie's touch upon her burned hands, and managed a faint smile. "If you can breach the barricade of my devoted nurses, sir, I shall be happy to welcome you."

For a moment the Viscount hesitated in the door and it seemed that he might, after all, decide not to go. But the moment passed, and pulling on his gloves with brisk decisiveness, he stepped out into the darkened hallway.

Finally at liberty to relax her control, Sarah threw one apologetic glance at Aggie before sinking back into the blissful oblivion of unconsciousness.

SEVENTEEN

"Her ladyship is sleeping, my lord." Aggie planted her wiry figure uncompromisingly across the entrance to her mistress's bedchamber. "She needs all the rest she can get, with that wicked cousin of hers still out to get her. Besides, it's four o'clock in the morning, which is a heathen time to be waking an invalid." She glared belligerently at the silent Viscount, ignoring the sheepish squirmings of Jem, her brother, who remained at his guard post outside the bedroom door. "Who's going to protect 'er, if I don't look out for 'er, that's what I want to know?"

"Your concern is very touching, Aggie," said the Viscount dryly. "Although I think I liked it better when you were more obsequious. But since I have already slain the dragon—metaphorically speaking—do you not think I might now be allowed to cast an eye upon the sleeping princess?"

"What do you mean, slain the dragon?" asked Aggie. "Have you been and gone and killed the Baron?"

"I admit I was tempted," said the Viscount, "but I decided, with some regret I may say, that our purposes would be better served if I did not go around London pumping bullets into the hearts of my wife's only remaining relatives. I simply persuaded the Baron that his life would be more comfortable, and much safer, if he sailed out of England on tomorrow's tide. He is not likely to brave the shores of this country again, I think."

"Well," Aggie sounded slightly mollified. "It's certainly a pleasure to hear that there's one villain the less to worry my Miss Sarah."

"Surely I am not still considered a villain, Aggie? Have I not yet redeemed any of my past errors in your eyes?"

"There's too many mysteries left for my liking," said Aggie bluntly. "I'm not saying you're in league with that 'orrible man in Streatham, but I'd still like to know how come you was so anxious to be a widower that you was picking a bride out of the poorhouse."

If the Viscount's feelings had not been so severely ruffled by Aggie's brusque question, he would have seen that the patient in the huge bed suddenly stiffened. As it was, he remained unaware of the extra pair of ears waiting eagerly for his answer.

"It is not my custom to explain my actions to a servant," began the Viscount stiffly, and then he caught himself up. "No," he said abruptly. "It is only fair for you to know what happened. My actions reflect little credit on my judgment, but I don't think even so stern a moralist as yourself could consider them villainous."

"That's as maybe, my lord. 'Tis hard to think what you was doin' there all the same."

"Aggie, my father left a ridiculous will that said I should inherit the family fortune only if I married within a year of his death. The will also stipulated that I should not marry a particular lady who—at the time—seemed very important to me. I went to the workhouse to find a woman who was dying. I wanted to marry somebody, anybody, just to meet the terms of my father's will. Then, when I had come into my inheritance and my workhouse bride had died, I planned to marry this other lady who, I thought, was my irrevocable choice. It was not a pretty scheme, I admit, but I am two-and-thirty and too old to submit well to an irrational whim of my father's. Am I forgiven, Aggie? You know, I am sure, that my plans changed weeks ago. As soon as I began to know Sarah, in fact."

"Well, it's not exactly what her sainted uncle would have wished," said Aggie dubiously. "But there's no denying that the Reverend was a man what ought never to have left the angels."

There was a small chuckle from the bed. "I think, my lord, that you are almost forgiven. I don't know how you have achieved the miracle. Sending a wicked baron fleeing from the country and wrapping us all in the most outrageous luxury would normally make no more than a slight dent in Aggie's armour-plated heart."

"Sarah!" Swiftly the Viscount crossed to her side. "You are supposed to be sleeping, not listening to me getting quite the worst of an argument with your former housekeeper."

Sarah's grey eyes smiled at him. "But I have been losing all my arguments with her for years! It makes you seem quite one of the family to hear you receiving the sharp edge of Aggie's tongue." She lifted one of her bandaged hands and winced as it rested against the Viscount's arm. "But seriously, my lord. Tell me, has he . . . has he truly gone?"

The Viscount's eyes softened as he gently stroked her arm. "I persuaded Baron Tynsdale that he was looking forward to a long stay abroad and that he really did not wish to pack more than one portmanteau. He left his cottage hastily with one of the servants still stuffing silver candlesticks into a sack. I did undertake to settle his affairs here in England, and to pay him a small quarterly sum from your estate. I fancy that he is a man who would not dream of risking such a guaranteed income merely to have the pleasure of seeing his native land. I think it is most unlikely that we shall be seeing him again."

"And very pleased I am to hear that," said Aggie austerely. "I never did understand how your sainted Mama came to have such a nasty set of relatives."

"It happens to the best of us," said the Viscount, sounding amused. "Particularly to the best of us, as a matter of fact. And with such paragons of virtue for a father and an uncle, I should have felt myself sadly out of place if Sarah had not had a few slightly less honourable relatives lurking in the background."

"You are too kind," said Sarah. "I'm sure your family

black sheep have so far stopped short of murder."

"In the last few generations at least," agreed the Viscount. "But I can assure you that our progression from Elizabethan yeomen to Stuart noblemen would not bear very close examination."

Sarah laughed, but she was still too tired to think of anything appropriate to say, and a slight silence fell over the occupants of the room. Even Aggie seemed temporarily at a loss for a word. It was the Viscount who finally broke the lengthening silence.

"Perhaps, Aggie, you would be good enough to fetch the Viscountess a hot drink?"

"But I have already had hot milk, and a cup of lemon juice mixed with honey," protested Sarah.

"Nevertheless, I think we need some more milk," said the Viscount, inexorably.

"Yes, my lord." Aggie seemed remarkably subdued, and retreated from the room without a backward glance.

"Whatever has come over her?" asked Sarah.

"Nothing very disastrous," said the Viscount dryly. "She is merely more adept than you are yourself in perceiving the symptoms of a man very much at the end of his tether."

"Do you mean you are tired, my lord?"

"Not precisely. So far during the course of this long and tempestuous day, however, I have survived an attempt to render me unconscious with laudanum; I have imagined you eloping with an unknown lover; I have fled unsuccessfully to your rescue—you have not yet heard that story—and I have chased a murdering scoundrel on to the road to Dover. Through all these multifarious activities, I have basically been thinking of only one thing."

"What is that, my lord?" whispered Sarah.

The Viscount's lips hovered tantalizingly close to Sarah's mouth. "It was this," he said as he kissed her, gently at first and then with a passion that startled them both.

"I cannot imagine that Aggie would be so undiplomatic as

to return with the milk," said the Viscount softly. "But in case she should contemplate such an indiscretion, I had better lock the door."

"It is very late," suggested Sarah tentatively. "Perhaps you ought to be sleeping."

"It is certainly late," agreed the Viscount equably. "It is almost morning, in fact. There would hardly be time to fall comfortably asleep before somebody would be waking me up in order to eat breakfast. I am sure there must be better ways to spend the next two or three hours."

His lips brushed a path of burning sensation along the side of her cheeks and down on to her shoulders. "Could you not help me to find some of them?" he asked.

Sarah rested her head against the comforting strength of the Viscount's shoulder.

"Yes, my lord," she whispered as he clasped her tight against his heart. "I am almost certain that I can."

Masquerade
Historical Romances

THE BLACK MARQUIS
by Margot Holland

After her father and betrothed are killed at the Battle of
Hastings, the lovely Saxon Lady Elfrida is left defenceless.
She journeys to the court at London – to find that King
William has bestowed her hand on the arrogant man
known as the Black Marquis. But the proud Elfrida is
not so easily won . . .

DEVIL'S KIN
by Anne Herries

Hester Stanley runs away to become mistress of a man she
hardly knows. Living in pre-Revolution Paris, she is
blissfully happy with Beau Vane – until doubts begin to
emerge . . . Why does Beau claim to be the Devil's brother?
And, above all, why will Beau not marry her?

Look out for these titles in your local paperback shop from
11th December 1981